'We have to love men a lot. A lot, a lot. Love them a lot in order to love them. Otherwise it's impossible; we couldn't bear them.'

Marguerite Duras

'Over the ocean, so they say,
beneath the sky, and far away,
there is a town
of mystical renown
and on the evening breeze
beneath vast dark trees
all my hope flees'

Josephine Baker

PRAISE FOR *MEN*

'Marie Darrieussecq brilliantly explores female anxiety about the masculine, and the desire for the masculine— always such a mysterious thing for a woman—whether he is black or white. This radical otherness takes us to the heart of what it means to be a woman.' *Télérama*

'From Los Angeles to Cameroon, via Paris, Marie Darrieussecq's novel is constantly on the edge of the fictional and the documentary. Romantic and creative passions merge with political and ethical visions...The character of Solange is the embodiment of a desire to grasp everything, in the intensity of the moment—and the same spirit animates Marie Darrieussecq's writing.'
Le Magazine Littéraire

'The issue of otherness is crucial, as is that of the couple. Are the characters a couple, or are they just the sum of one another? This novel and its romance is a surprise from Marie Darrieussecq, but she proves herself to be, as ever, a socially aware writer.' *Paris Match*

'The film shoot in Cameroon is a piece of bravura writing... pages that take your breath away...Jungle fever, the attraction between people from different races—is the jungle here metaphoric or real?' *Le Nouvel Observateur*

'Darrieussecq revisits the clash of civilisations, of two worlds, one supposedly civilised, the other immersed in the heart of darkness...Without a single cliché or platitude, this novelist chooses to contrast a mythical Africa with that of harsh reality.' *Jeune Afrique*

'If it weren't for her prose, which is like a brooding snake— sharp, sometimes dissonant, twisting—Marie Darrieussecq's new novel would remind you of one of those slice-of-life films, ultra anti-romantic, no emotional clap-trap...And this novel is all about the cinema...It's a novel-film.' *Le Point*

PRAISE FOR MARIE DARRIEUSSECQ,
TOM IS DEAD AND *ALL THE WAY*

'There are few writers who may have changed my perception
of the world, but Darrieussecq is one of them.' *The Times*

'The internationally celebrated author who illuminates those parts
of life other writers cannot or do not want to reach.' *Independent*

'"To say what is not said, that is the point of writing,"
claims Darrieussecq. And that is exactly what this novel,
All the Way, does as it shatters taboos, over-simplifications
and affectations.' *Le Magazine Littéraire*

'I absolutely adored this account of a sexual awakening.' *L'Express*

'Preoccupied with what is both strange yet familiar,
this clever novel, *All the Way*, is both personal and universal
—and without the slightest trace of sentimentality.' *Libération*

'*Tom Is Dead* is powerful; when one has finished reading it
one feels it absolutely needed to exist.' *Nancy Huston*

'*Tom Is Dead* is mesmerising and deeply rewarding....
impressive in its evocation of vastly different worlds and lives.'
Australian Literary Review

'Darrieussecq is as daring as she is original...
a singular new voice.' *Irish Times*

'She makes all those daring young men of letters
look very tame indeed.' *Herald* (Glasgow)

'Another astonishing work by Darrieussecq. *All the Way* is
a stunning achievement.' M. J. HYLAND

'Her gifts are dazzling.' *Observer*

'I love the way Marie Darrieussecq writes about the world
as if it were an extension of herself and her feelings.'
J.M.G LE CLEZIO, Nobel Laureate for Literature 2008

'As ever, Marie Darrieussecq is a step ahead.' *Sunday Telegraph*

'*All the Way* is a darkly comic work that is likely to cause outrage and indignation from the usual quarters...Darrieussecq highlights literature's ability to explore the dark corners of our own collective box of secrets, in which children are neither as naïve nor as oblivious as we wish to believe.' *Monthly*

'Explicit, funny and unsentimental, *All the Way* captures what it's like to be underage and out of your mind with desire. Darrieussecq is a sublime writer with real insight.' *Sydney Morning Herald*

'At the heart of her gripping new novel is the thorny territory of adolescence and its raging loneliness, as a young French girl determines to go all the way sexually. The beautiful translation succeeds in capturing the nuances of the protagonist, the ultra-sensitive Solange, and her kaleidoscope of teenage thought and emotion...Darrieussecq's storytelling keeps the reader engaged all the way, too.' *Australian*

'The French *enfant terrible* Marie Darrieussecq has been much overlooked in Anglophone circles—a scandal.' *The Times*

'A dreamy and daring narrative.' *Courier Mail*

'A sharp, funny and honest description of a girl coming to grips with her blooming sexuality.' *Herald Sun*

'Darrieussecq is not afraid to break social taboos, nor does she flinch from the utter selfishness that accompanies adolescence...sad, funny and challenging.' *Otago Daily Times*

'In *All the Way*, Darrieussecq dissects with anatomical precision the climate of small-town France in the 1980s, with its strange mix of sexual openness and the continued prevalence of a particularly French brand of chauvinism and racism, all coloured by the disappointment of a generation that came of age in 1968, the promised revolution having faded almost completely, leaving nothing more noble than a petit bourgeois sensibility.'
Times Literary Supplement

MARIE DARRIEUSSECQ was born in 1969 in Bayonne, France. Her novel *Pig Tales* was published in thirty-four countries. She lives in Paris. Text has also published *Tom Is Dead* and *All the Way*.

PENNY HUESTON is an editor and translator.

Men

Marie Darrieussecq

TRANSLATED FROM THE
FRENCH BY PENNY HUESTON

TEXT PUBLISHING MELBOURNE AUSTRALIA

textpublishing.com.au

The Text Publishing Company (UK) Ltd
130 Wood Street, London EC2V 6DL, United Kingdom

The Text Publishing Company
Swann House, 22 William Street, Melbourne, Victoria 3000, Australia

Il faut beaucoup aimer les hommes was originally published French in 2013 by P.O.L éditeur.
This edition published by The Text Publishing Company in 2016.

Page and cover design by W.H. Chong
Typeset by J&M Typesetters

Printed in Australia by Griffin Press, an accredited ISO/NZS 14001:2004 Environmental Management System printer

9781925240917 (Australian paperback)
9781911231028 (UK paperback)
9781922253538 (ebook)

National Library of Australia Cataloguing-in-Publication entry:
Creator: Darrieussecq, Marie, author.
Title: Men/by Marie Darrieussecq;
translated from the French by Penny Hueston.
Subjects: Man-woman relationships—Fiction. Race relations—Fiction.
Blacks—Race identity—Fiction. Whites—Race identity—Fiction.
Stereotypes (Social psychology)—Fiction.
Other Creators/Contributors: Hueston, Penny, translator.
Dewey Number: 843.914

You go by sea and reach a river. You can take a plane, of course. But you reach a river and you have to enter the river. Sometimes there's a port, and cranes, cargo ships, sailors. And lights at night. A port on the habitable section of the delta. After that there's no one. Only trees, as you head up the river.

OPENING CREDITS

He was a man with a big idea. She could see it shining in his eyes. His pupils coiled into incandescent ribbons. She sank into his gaze to follow the river with him. But she didn't believe in his project. It would never happen for real. Does anyone ever make it to the Congo?

That was the thing about him: he was a problem. And his big idea cost too much money. Expected too much from too many people. And for her the big idea was like another woman in his life.

'From brooding too long on the Congo/ I have become a Congo resounding with forests and rivers/ where the whip cracks like a great banner.' He read to her from Césaire. Who was not her favourite writer. But who left us some decent pages, there's no denying it. And who was black, which carries some weight. Arguably. From then on, she came from there, too. From an impossible, cataclysmic, teeming country.

Every morning she woke up afflicted with a skin disease. Her shoulders, her breasts, the insides of her arms, anything that came in contact with him—her skin was ruptured with an embroidery of encrusted lines that were spreading. She rubbed and scrubbed but they didn't go away. She showered but the water made no difference, and in the mirror she could see, beneath the skin, patterns of narrow tunnels, of delicate, hollowed-out pearl necklaces.

Even the make-up artist couldn't do anything for her. And she was supposed to play the role of the diaphanous French woman, no tattoos, no marks. You can't see your own face. Nor your back, granted. If you twist around, you catch a glimpse of shoulderblade, a bit of collarbone and the small of your back. But you carry your face in front of you like an offering. He saw her. She only saw herself in films or in the mirror. That flawless face, on which marks were even more visible.

And who was he? An actor like her, supporting roles, not that well known—his face was familiar, but not his name, which was hard to pronounce. If he had a radical streak in him, it manifested itself in his determination to keep his name—to make a career with a name like that. A name that she, too, would have liked to go by. She imagined combining it with her own typically French first name, Solange.

2

He didn't like her looking at him when they made love. If she opened her eyes, he went *shhhh*. She shut them again; she went back inside the red darkness. But she had seen his face, overcome with emotion, his cheeks radiant, the sweat on his cheekbones, like tears. And his eyes fixed on her, *shhhh*. Two black pinpoints, staring out from under his eyelids, his Chinese eyes, two slits, beneath his triangular forehead.

She remembered his beauty geometrically, but who was the man in the photograph? Who was the man whose picture was in all the Hollywood gossip magazines? Who was the man who used to look at her, who, in her memory, is looking at her now? Her skin no longer bears any trace of him, only the imprint of time, the scars from film shoots that she seems to have dreamt up.

PART I

THE BEGINNING

The beginning is like an incision. She is forever revisiting the beginning; it stands out distinctly in the course of her life, whereas what follows seems back to front, or cut off, or in disarray.

She saw him, only him. At one of George's parties. Most of the guests were there, but she entered a magnetic field. A denser sphere of air that excluded everyone else. She was silent. In his presence she was reduced to silence and solitude. She could not speak: she had nothing to say. A palpable, dazzling force field radiated from him, a blast from a contained explosion. A wave coursed through her and she disintegrated. Her atoms were pulverised. She was in suspension and, already, that's what she wanted: disintegration.

He was wearing a strange coat, long, made of delicate,

flowing material. He wasn't looking at her. He was looking at the base of the canyon, at the lights of Los Angeles. His demeanour, his dark head, was unfathomable, as if the effort required by his own bearing completely preoccupied him. As if he were the only human being present who was aware of the burden that is a head. Backlit by the lanterns, his long hair was outlined in a deep cowl and his slender silhouette gave him a monastic air. The intensity of the force field became such that one of them—she—pronounced a few words, about the balmy evening, or George, or whatever they were drinking, and it was like taking a breath. The night turned pale in the fog; a watery haze formed over them. He rolled her a cigarette. Their hands did not touch, but there was such a brutal strengthening of the force field that the cigarette floated, passed between them without their knowing how, in the vibrating, humming space. In the dark, he mimed looking for a lighter in the bottomless pockets of his coat. He didn't have one—no, he did—the flame erupted. She burned her hair leaning in too close and she laughed, mistakenly, as he was already silently demanding the utmost seriousness from her. She took a drag and surfaced for air, one last time.

Then she plunged into the core of the world, with him, into the force field, into the fog that was choking Laurel Canyon, into total happiness, impenetrable and white—disintegration.

*

He was a phenomenal actor. He had the ability to call up different lives, right before him, around him, metamorphosed, one on top of the other, and never bogus. It was him, multiplied. He had reached the level of self-confidence to be himself in role after role, like George or Nicole or Isabelle. But he had never reached star status. And yet, as she witnessed later, he inspired adoration, fear and neediness.

At first she thought he was American. His intonation, the way he moved. An eccentric American, for sure, but in the Hollywood Hills you dress however you like. As for her, everyone knew she was French. She could work on her accent and play an American, but most of the time they wanted her to play a French woman: the shrill bitch, the elegant ice queen, the romantic victim. Wearing Chanel and Louboutin outfits, which she got to keep after the shoot.

He would play a drug dealer or a boxer, sometimes a cop or a priest or the best friend of the broad-minded hero. He had been a low-profile Jedi in an episode of *Star Wars*. In real life he played an American like everyone else, like he had played Hamlet when he first started out. With the same quiet intensity. The same focused indifference. At the Bouffes du Nord theatre, when she was at the Paris Conservatory, it could only have been him. His voice was muted and deep, his torso enormous, broad shoulders on a long body, which she could only guess at because he was wearing a kind of cloak. His voice seemed to emanate from deep in his throat, beneath that soft hollow spot where the neck begins and where she would so love to kiss him, later, asking him if he was annoyed by her feelings for him, and he would reply: 'Why would I be annoyed?'

His *t*s had a soft, mellow fullness, scarcely different from his *d*s, which at first she took to be the affectation of a handsome man and an actor—the way certain aristo-crats speak in France—whereas for him it indicated his background. In her case, people often joked that, even from a satellite, you could tell she was French. Was it her figure? The angle of her jawline? Or the tic of starting sentences with a little sceptical pout? Apparently, languages shape faces. Her speech therapist in Los Angeles, with whom she practised accents, thought it was an issue of muscular tension.

Yes, she was French. He had been to Paris. He liked Paris, the historical buildings. Yes, it's a beautiful city. How long had she been in Los Angeles? Four years (she pretended to think about it), one-two-three-four, since 2003. Ever since her son had chosen to live with his father—she felt the urge to tell him that, although nothing in his tall figure, in his unfathomable demeanour, in the absence of a smile, invited the sharing of confidences. He had asked about Los Angeles for other reasons. To chat about their careers, in fact. He was silent; she remained silent. Already, she was following his lead. She had just grasped that he was not American. Once she had confirmed that she was French, he had revealed another accent, perhaps another way of behaving. He was Canadian. Which did not completely satisfy her. But she didn't press for more. Not immediately. She would rather have been consumed in a flash, like vampires startled by daylight, than claim to reduce him to the matter of his origins. They were two strangers, two adopted Americans. Two strangers also oddly familiar to each other. As if they knew each other already through intervening countries. As if the intensity of that day was also the logical, electrical consequence of history's detonation system.

The coyotes were yapping in the hills, close by. They came to drink from the swimming pools. Their call was more like a wailing, not at all like a wolf, more like some kind of freakish baby. George eventually came over, a bottle of Cristal in his hand. He had just been in a science-fiction film and bits of the set, like the cosmically white armchairs, had been reused for the party. He seemed, as ever, to have fallen from heaven, in an immaculate suit, with his tanned complexion, and his smile like the Milky Way. He introduced them to each other, first names only, as if it was obvious, as if they were as famous as he was. That's how classy George was. With him everything became normal again: the gigantic turquoise swimming pool, the hundred-odd guests, the steamy night in the hills, and that looming man's impossible first name, like bones grating. And two days later she would realise that he hadn't heard her name at all.

They were whisked away by a group of people, George's gravitational field. There was Kate, and Mary, and Jen, and Colin, and Lloyd, and Ted, and two or three of Steven's friends and also that girl who was in *Collateral Damage*. A beautiful ethnic girl, as they say in France, Puerto Rican perhaps. Heads bobbing, shadows fluttering. She was looking around for him in the dark. She did not dare scrutinise his face, his impassive Jedi countenance. Earlier she had made an effort to look away, like him, at the hills, at the flame of the lighter up close, or at the Great Bear far away. And that actress, the Puerto Rican, there was something odd about her gaze, a sort of squint—yes, she was ogling him; she did not take her eyes off him, whereas everyone else was staring at George, at his white silhouette in the light.

The Puerto Rican goes up to him. He bursts out laughing, their heads bobbing; she can't see them for the shadows. Now Steven is coming over to Solange. She mimes a phone, two fingers against her ear: she'll call him later. She doesn't want to talk to Steven; she wants to talk to *him*. His laughter is the only sound in the hubbub. His face split in two by dazzling teeth—everyone has dazzling teeth; it would be inconceivable for them not to have dazzling teeth here. But that laughter unleashes the night, divides the fog; the galactic prince's mouth is split in two by the laughter intended for the Puerto Rican girl. Solange sees only the dazzling whiteness of their sixty-four teeth.

'Are you from Puerto Rico?'

The alleged Puerto Rican girl turns to Solange. Examines her. 'I am from Los Angeles,' she replies, dazzling. 'Aren't we all from LA?' *LA*—she drags out the long vowel,

Ellaaay...and Solange realises who she is, Lola something, a rising starlet, born in Suriname. She was in *Lost*—God knows what the scriptwriters lined up for her, devoured by a bear or crushed in a rift in the cosmos—but in any case she is at that stage of notoriety where *everyone* is supposed to know that she hacked her way out, with a machete, from her native jungle to the Hollywood Hills.

Bottles of Cristal are brought around on silver platters. The prince in the long coat is contemplating Los Angeles, or the night, or whatever is on his mind—this man with the unfathomable demeanour—and she wants to know what that is.

A tidal motion swings them back towards the swimming pool suspended above the canyon. The sea is a long, opaque line. He turns his head towards her. Slowly. It's almost imperceptible at first. At the end of the movement he holds her eyes in his gaze. Then—keeping his eye line perfectly horizontal—he looks back at the sea. It was so brief, so precise, that she is not sure if it happened.

Floria and Lilian arrive and greet Ted and kiss Solange. She mumbles a brief introduction. Ted looks at the man of the brief introduction, then looks at her. Another bottle of Cristal materialises. The party ebbs and flows, like a wave, the circles open and close, she battles the currents. A little island has formed once more and she is alone with him, against the guardrail above the canyon.

A TIGER DEFYING THE LAWS OF GRAVITY

They do not say anything. The silence is marvellous. If you have ever found yourself in a substantial residence, high up, protected from the sea but with a full panorama; if you have had the chance to experience that silence and that sense of security, you will know what deep calm…you will know how Los Angeles…and them, both minuscule and gigantic up above the canyon, and the city, lying low, spread out, turbulent and glowing.

He stayed there with her, on the pretext of sharing the bottle. Instead of following the group around George and Lola. Instead of following Steven or Ted or some other purveyor of roles and fortune and fame. Or, at the very least, of a stimulating conversation. Or of some decent cocaine. He stays with her. She has known him forever and is getting to know him second by second: it is *here and now*, just the right moment in life, taking a risk on adventure, good times, the union of the present and the ever-after. She is drunk. They discover similar interests.

He likes to read. She plucks up her courage and laughs for real. 'There's nothing more sexy than a man who reads.' She would like to elaborate. She would like to explain to him—as he leans in, alone, needing no one, caught up in a crowd but with his unfathomable head held high, a smile to light up his entrance, his welcome interruption: hello, hello, my love. She would have so many things to tell him. So many things to explain to him. He is reading for a project he's working on. He reads a lot on set. 'All those actors who want to stay focused between takes, all that fuss about the Actors Studio, what a joke.' He gives a short laugh. The two of them are not American. He reads at night. She pictures him wrapped in a white sheet, naked to the waist and hunched forwards, his long hair slipping over the book. He recites the names of writers she has never heard of; she catches the two syllables of Conrad and whips out some French names. He doesn't pick up on it. But he stays there.

The silence unfolds, changes direction. He smells good. She wants to touch him. He smells like a church, like an Indian temple. The moon has risen. The sea has expanded, black and starless, a second sky. She racks her brains for something to say. She would like to say that she came to Los Angeles for the sea. In Paris the sea was too far away; even when she was small she missed the sea. But he won't believe her. Especially coming from an actress. He is standing in profile against the charcoal-grey sky. Between her and the sea there is only him. She can look at him just by raising her eyes. A high, rounded forehead. Some kind of grooves in his skin: she can't tell in this light. Scars? Invisible eyes, slits. A long, thin nose, aquiline. Large lips, firmly closed, well defined. How does it happen, why do these particular elements form such consummate beauty?

She thinks back to early school drawings: 2, and 4, and 6…by lining up the numbers in a column you produced a strange, bumpy shape. She can hear him breathing in the silence. He doesn't like chatterboxes, it must be that. Or explanations. He likes to go at his own pace. Or else it is all in her own head, and the city is nothing but a projection; she thinks she has been living there for four years but all she does is float on the surface. She tries to cling to the illusion that her feet are grounded, that the vibrations she feels are part of the city of Los Angeles itself. She would like to tell him about the week when a huge image of her face was displayed on a billboard, at the intersection of Sunset Boulevard and La Cienega Boulevard, for the launch of *Musette*. There were so many things she could say about it, say to him, that would be unexpected, witty. Not at all what he imagines, not at all like other actresses. She asks him for another glass of champagne.

'I like the way you say *champagne*,' he says. 'It's so chic, so French.' She laughs. He makes fun of the American accent: 'They say *champayne* like *John Wayne*.' She laughs again. Every word he says is precious, reveals a little more behind his unfathomable demeanour. His eyes reveal nothing. Perhaps he saw her in *Musette*. Perhaps he's got a thing for French girls, the usual thing.

A few people walk back towards them. Of all these bipeds only George and he know how to carry with elegance our lot as upright creatures. Everyone else uses cigarettes, glasses or studied gestures in order to keep their hands beside their bodies. Those two are simply upright on Earth. He reminds her of someone but it's not George, despite their shared elegance. She casts about, compares the nose, the mouth, but it's more about the look, or the stature...or, she's not sure, a strong sense of self, a powerful torso, the neck a Greek pillar—a statue from antiquity, the human race, all in one.

*

They head towards the cars. George takes the keys out of her hand: there is apparently no question of her driving. George's limousine turns into a deluxe minibus. He is not far from her, two seats away, two bodies away. George speaks to the chauffeur before they set off and Ted, who works for George in his production company, settles in next to her. A joint does the rounds. The starlet is chatting with Steven (what on earth will Solange's agent, Lloyd, say when he finds out that she told Steven, the famous Steven, that she'd call him back). She should go to bed early. They're driving along a boulevard; it's been four years but she still gets them muddled, whatever, it must be Hollywood Boulevard. They're outside the Chinese Theatre, the starlet knows a nightclub, the Montmartre Lounge—unbelievable, she pronounces *Montt-martt-re* with *t*s everywhere. Solange wants to keep passing the joint but no one is paying any attention, so she smokes it with Ted. George has left. And Steven. Next thing there are bright lights and lots of people and an old Queen hit single and Freddy Mercury's razor-sharp voice: he's a star leaping through the skies *like a tiger defying the laws of gravity.*

Because of the joint each syllable is enunciated, the drums detach from the piano and the piano from the guitar and the guitar from the voice, all the trajectories divide and reunite: celestial harmony. She has never particularly liked Queen but she remembers an anecdote, well, an interesting fact, she starts shouting in his ear—he's tall but she has very high heels—that Freddy Mercury was a Parsi, a what, a Parsi—how do you say Parsi in English, *Parsi* sounds just fine—in any case she's off and running: a fascinating religion, sun worshippers, strict vegans, they don't bury their dead but perform an extremely civilised ritual—he asks her to repeat, she shouts at the top of her voice: they lay them out on the top of towers, the Towers of Silence—she's yelling— the vultures come and devour them; it takes twenty-odd vultures ten minutes to reduce the bodies to perfectly white bones, which are then arranged in the tower, in circles, in a super-sophisticated system, gutters and drains for the bodily fluids, so clean, much more hygienic than burial when you think about it. The problem is that there are almost no vultures in Bombay anymore because of the pollution, so the neighbouring Hindus complain about the bodies.

'Interesting,' he says.

It looks like he thinks it is. It's perhaps not the ideal conversation but he's looking her in the eye. They step aside at the same time to get clear of the music, which is every-where, she can't hear a word he's saying, the image of the decomposing bodies is sort of floating between them—'I've heard'—she scarcely changes the subject—'that elephants are the only animals to have a ritual for their dead.' She is full of hope. Hope that he might talk to her. The elephants are swaying from side to side, rocking the white bones of their comrades in their trunks. Hope that he might explain things to her, take her away, carry her off elephant-style. But his face is impassive again. Almost stony.

'I know nothing about elephants,' he replies dryly.

'I know a lot about Parsis.' She laughs feebly.

He is still wearing his improbable Jedi coat and drops of sweat are pearling at the roots of his hair; it's either the heat of the nightclub or a sort of annoyance that she can't identify, exhaustion, a kind of impatience, pity for her. She wouldn't have believed it, but perhaps he's one of those men with whom you have to make the first move.

There is a slippage in time and space, a plunge forward and she's dancing with Ted. Donna Summer pants and moans and whispers *ooooohhh I feel love I feel love I feel love.* Ted is irrelevant but at least he's acting normally, normally for someone whose nose is white with powder. He sways his hips, holds out his hand, caresses her shoulder, mouthing the lyrics, and she spins around. The Canadian Jedi is standing at the bar, motionless, staring into space. Under the tilting lights she watches him move away across the dance floor towards the exit—she has to follow him; she has no choice. The perfumed flapping of his big coat envelops her; she hears Ted's voice tinged with bitterness: 'You're heading for trouble.'

TROUBLE

She's running. He's three metres behind her and the roar of the bullets is terrifying. The clatter of her extremely high heels echoes in her head, as if she were running beneath her own skull. The make-up is dry and crepey on her cheeks and she has a terrible urge to rub her eyes. He's running too fast; they've reached the marker on the left; he's too close; watch out for the marker on the right, the corner, the railing. Her lungs are going to explode. She throws herself into the green corner, she screams, Matt Damon jumps on her and the blood spurts, she pants, she dies—cut.

He was too close! Obviously the extra was too close; she's pretty sure he doesn't realise it's the cameras they're running for and not the film crew. Sixth take. It's little more than a form of slavery, at the mercy of digital ever since film stock became worthless. *You were great, Solange, you were superb, I love you.* The director overdoes it a bit. The make-up woman wipes off most of the blood before they head back to the dressing room where the props woman rants as she tears Solange's skin under the shirt. At least the wardrobe woman is an angel: she slipped her some padded inner soles for the stilettos, which didn't prevent her legs from turning into jackhammers. She needs a massage between takes. Matt is sure to get massages. Lloyd sold her the role by telling her that she would die *in the arms of Matt Damon.* In the end, their interaction is nothing more than a knee jab (from him) in the chest (hers). On the first take the damn blood sachet refused to burst; she's a battered actress.

Her phone is still showing no messages.

The wardrobe woman cuts the shirt off with scissors so as not to interfere with the wig; the hairdresser sprays the wig with lacquer; the make-up artist covers her eyes and redoes the foundation. She looks awful, terrifying. And there are marks on her face. The make-up artist is working hard on the under-eye concealer. The props person returns with a sixth sachet of blood. She has to change her bra, but Olga from wardrobe doesn't have any more in her size. They unwrap a sixth shirt, Olga gives it a quick iron while Natsumi, the assistant, runs off to buy a bra—it's not *Danger in Malibu*; she's not going to tear around without one. Phones are ringing left, right and centre. Except hers.

Perhaps he didn't find the Post-it note she left him

with her number on it? Or else he's still sleeping—this late? They're saying that number two camera didn't reverse at the right time. Mobile phones are vibrating full bore, about to fly off the tables. She turns hers off and restarts it: it's working. Natsumi returns empty-handed, red and sweaty. No B-cup bras: apparently she's the only female in this city to have kept a normal breast size. Outside, everyone's screaming. No one has eaten yet. She's not sure whether to call her place on the landline. If he's still there, would he pick up? He was fast asleep and she hesitated over her note, the Post-it note pad in her hand: *There's coffee, honey and cereal, I'm leaving my keys so you can lock up, give them to the concierge, or call me to return them, here's my number…*She looked at him as he slept. In the rays of fluorescent light from the street. She crossed out *to return them.*

Give them to the concierge or call me, whatever suits you…

Whatever suits you sounded like a prayer. In the end she just stuck her number on the coffee pot, the keys and honey in front.

'Olga, could you call me, please?' Olga does as she's asked: the phone works.

Kale salads have been delivered. It's hard to chew. The make-up artist says that kale contains much larger amounts of raphanin than broccoli and is wonderful for the complexion.

It would be easy enough to ask George for his number. But that's out of the question. Anyway, she wouldn't even know how to pronounce his name.

She remembers Bob Evans, the producer, who asked his housekeeper to slip a note under his morning coffee cup with the first name of the girl in his bed. And she remembers Michelle Pfeiffer in *Catwoman*, in her lonely little apartment, interrogating her answering machine in vain.

Olga waves a bra under her nose. It's Natsumi's own bra, a Princess Tam Tam bra in her size, warm and slightly damp. She has time to lie down under a blanket before they call her—careful of the hair and make-up. They'll get her to put on the shirt at the last minute. There's a problem with the green corner, the one where they'll install the tunnel to interstellar space; it means rethinking the whole approach of the design. Does he take coffee or tea in the morning? She should have stuck the Post-it note on the kettle instead. Or on the bedside table?

They should have gone back to his place. He told her it was in Topanga. But that was too far. It's all for the best: he's waiting for her. He made himself some coffee. He studied the photos on the shelves, opened a few books. He went back to bed. He's reading. Did he notice the photo of her son? She wondered about removing it. He likes her home. He doesn't reply to the landline: it's not his place.

Her nipples are on fire and it's not the bra. When she was running she managed not to think about it. He was big, he enveloped her, his mouth on her breasts, his fingers in her hair, his hips against hers, almost swallowing her, inhaling her, taking all of her, and his hands grabbing her again, the back of her neck, her buttocks, his grip tight, lifting her up and holding her, squeezing her, sweeping her off her feet. Under the blanket she is burning up with electrical charges. It's an adrenaline-fuelled desire. Natsumi and Olga are silent in the steam from their green tea; they look like they're asleep. Have they, too, ever left pieces of themselves beside someone? On the deck chairs is a projection of Olga and Natsumi, a hologram; the real Olga and Natsumi are scattered in some unmade bed, in this city or somewhere else, in the wake of a man.

What's the matter with her? What's got into her? He had scars at the corners of his eyes, little triangles, clearly defined. She has retained everything about him, his gestures, words, smell, manner, style, and everything about his appearance that she could take away with her, his outer casing, the skin that enveloped and wrapped him, keeping him there. She was able to hold him in her arms, and she said to herself: he is here, with me, in me. Provisions for memory. Provisions for strength. Because already another force wanted him, she knew it, a force that would be trying to take him from her, always.

Olga, Natsumi, speak to me. Look at me. The strange and marvellous marks on my skin are proof that I wasn't dreaming—no, the proof is the incision, the waiting, the open road. Outlines of standing figures, superimposed images from films, straight, delineated roads, planes swooping over deserts, mazes to hide in, heat mirages over the occasional car…

'Solange. Wake up!'

It's Olga leaning over her—for a second she thought it was her mother, all hazy above her cradle, far away. Her phone: no messages. And in a few minutes she'll have to run in stilettos.

'You looked like you were fast asleep,' says Olga. 'Did you take something last night?'

VIDEO

The keys are where she left them. As well as the Post-it note with her number. And the concierge's greeting was perfectly natural. She knew immediately that he had left just like that, shut the door, no note, nothing.

The bed is unmade but there's nothing lying around, no clothes. He didn't make himself coffee. He didn't eat. Didn't touch anything. Didn't make himself at home.

He gets up, late. He gets dressed. He finds his way to the kitchen, which is also the way out. He sees the Post-it note.

At that point she can't work out what his expression is. She can't decipher it.

Or else he wakes when she leaves. He leaps up to catch her, but her taxi has already left. He lets the curtain fall shut again, goes back to bed, and grabs a pillow. He gently scratches his flat belly, his nose buried in the smell of her. He thinks about what they did together, what they said. Or else…

Or else he orders a taxi, waits at the entrance of the apartment block, chats to the concierge, and heads off somewhere, she has no idea where, perhaps in the direction of Topanga Canyon.

She is sore all over but she goes back out to see the concierge. They must have talked. They would have at least said hello to each other. The concierge is black, too.

That's the first time she's thought about it. Black, under the red cap. Did he see, did he notice this morning (he notices everything: it's his job), did a guy with a long coat come by? It feels like she's describing a thief. But she's not going to dwell on her private life. 'He used to be in that series, you know, *Connection.*' The series was very popular among African-Americans. And, anyway, a guy like that doesn't walk through a secure residential complex without being noticed. With his long coat.

But perhaps he had it folded under his arm. It was already hot this morning. She starts again. She is exhausted. Her night, her day, something has made her exhausted. 'A really tall guy, with long thin braids.' She knows perfectly well that they're called *dreadlocks*. But she can't do it. Not in front of the concierge. She has never said *dreadlocks* in her life. Or perhaps once, referring to Bob Marley. 'A tall guy with a coat. A coloured guy, wearing jeans.' There is not a single black person living in the apartment block. Or in the entire neighbourhood, now that she thinks about it. 'Coloured'—how ridiculous.

The concierge's inertia is getting on her nerves. She feels like asking him what is the point of being a concierge, asking him for the footage from the security cameras. To find out what time he left. What he looked like. What his expression was, his mood. She'd like—she doesn't know, really—to talk about him. For someone to tell her: 'I saw him. He's charismatic. Enigmatic. But what was apparent, as clear as day, was how much he was thinking about you.'

She would like to see him again.

She goes to YouTube and looks at clips from *Connection*. It's amazing. There he is, just like she saw him the first time. His voice. His gestures. Not his vocabulary, although he effortlessly delivers a string of *motherfuckers*. His presence. His glorious presence. Still radiating around her apartment. He was there, here, in her bed. The videos only last three minutes. She wonders about downloading a whole episode. She has to sleep: she's filming again tomorrow.

His name is there in the different sets of credits, with different spellings, but the most common is Kouhouesso Nwokam. Which is not all that complicated. She doesn't learn much online, nothing about his private life. On Wikipedia, his date of birth: if it's correct, he is two years older than her. A Canadian citizen born in English-speaking Cameroon. She had no idea there was an

English-speaking Cameroon. Google Images photos, some flattering, others where he is smiling broadly, which doesn't suit him, others where he is heavier and it suits him.

She jumps: the sound of a text message.

Natsumi. She forgot to return the bra.

A clip from a film that was very successful three or four years ago: *Dazed*. He plays a cop. It takes place in a house by the sea. His white colleague, the hero, interrogates a handcuffed dealer who swears at them. He doesn't do much: he's slightly in the shadows, but he'll get his turn. He's going to—no, not speak—but he turns slowly to the bay window. A veil of softness suddenly descends like a halo on the scene, a yellow, powdery light—a weary archangel shaking his wings. As if gazing into infinity, he stares out over the sea. The look of a bored cop, of an actor who is thinking. Beyond that place, beyond the film. He stares at the sea and she'd like to be the sea. He stares at the waves and she'd like to be the waves. She'd like to be the empty space, she'd like to be that place elsewhere, she'd like to be the song he has on his mind and she'd like him to sing it, sing her, let him drift off, yes, but in her direction. She'd like to be that wandering, absent thought, that aside of his in the film from three or four years ago.

He refocuses, back to the action, says the line they're waiting for. *Say something, motherfucker*, interrupts the white cop grandstanding as a psychologist, and crushes the head of the dealer against the table. It cuts out, she rewinds…there…

right at the moment he's turning towards the window…
there…he's bored…*good cop, bad cop*…he really is bored, he
stares at the sea, he's thinking about something else. And
the director has kept the take, he *saw*, that's why he makes
films, for moments like these, the moment when the film
slips away, taking advantage of a mistake, a moment of
detachment, of reverie, a shift—there: an actor stares at
the sea and his grace detonates the image…

The movement, the powdery light, the eyes on the
ocean.

It's like the other evening in the hills. Exactly the same
look, the same urgency, and it's unbearable, and she has to
live it, quickly.

SEE YOU ON THE OTHER SIDE

Words. She remembered his words as if he was whispering them, passionately, between her breasts.

Let me kiss you, let me kiss you again, I love kissing you, I love the taste of your lips. I don't want the morning to come.

But he's no longer there. And he hasn't called.

It happened in English. Perhaps it would not have registered with such force in French. Well, how would she know? The particular sentence that keeps coming back to her, his voice shuddering, could have been any sentence, but it was those words uttered with that voice: *I want to stay inside you forever.* How would you say a sentence like that in French? *Je veux rester à l'intérieur de toi pour toujours?*

She's running, in the racket of bullets and her high heels, and all she can hear are those words, and all she can feel is the jolt in her belly of each word coursing through her. Each flash of memory catches up with her, and her destination—the corner of green canvas where she has to collapse, where Matt Damon will suddenly appear—that corner is a resting point, her thoughts stop, her suffocating brain and pounding legs clamour for a bit of basic, physical attention, and she catches her breath as she pretends to be in agony. Words, snatches of them, mantras. And she is back in that night again, a single night, far bigger than she is.

The director thinks she's *wild, sublime, you're sublime, Solange, you're wild.*

He had fallen asleep straight away, into a deep sleep. It is rare for her to sleep with someone, and she had not anticipated sleeping with him. She looked at his face. She could look at him, knowing that he would probably hate it. Long and thin in profile, surprisingly broad face-on. Not the same man face-on and in profile.

She wanted to kiss his lips, his nose, the roots of his hair, the strange little triangles scored into the corners of his eyes. His large soft neck, the skin slightly wrinkled. The sturdy collarbone joints, the curve of his shoulders, his arms, his chest. His soft skin, tensile, smooth, thick, perfectly defining his contours, his muscles, his tendons, with the exception of his soft neck, where she glimpsed his age. A man asleep inside his strength, moulded by his skin.

A few minutes earlier, she had uttered some words, too. She said: *I love your skin.* And it was true, she adored it, she kissed it and caressed it, thick, supple, smooth, those words from her mouth a kiss alighting, a butterfly.

He had flinched, loosened his embrace, moved away ever so slightly, but it was a huge distance, a huge distance from his skin to hers. He had said: *I know nothing about skin.*

Skin is contact. That's what she meant, that's all. The softness of their skin, rubbing against each other, coupled: that contact.

He had taken her in his arms again; she was absolved, embraced, as if he approved of her reply. And he fell asleep (she is being grabbed by Matt Damon, who is grinding his knee between her breasts, and the blood is spurting), and she had been able to look at him. Gaze at him. He was copper-brown, chocolate, the hollow in his neck almost black, the palms of his hands almost red, the soles of his feet orange; and she was pale beige, bluish around the wrists, pale pink breasts, mauve-brown nipples, a slightly green bruise on her sternum. She was white and she didn't know it.

They're doing another take, straight away, from the top, Matt and Solange, the spurting blood, Hollywood. She says her line, in an exaggerated French accent: *See you on the other side.* Her only line, but it's the title of the film. He flings himself into the green corner and you'll see, in the cinema, it will be the spectacular entrance into a rift in the space-time continuum and she will be lying there on the threshold, dead.

From the top, again. Matt sits himself on her chest

34

again, the bullet's fired, she's dying. Natsumi rearranges her outfit, Damon's pelvis is right in front of her mouth—it's weird, but she does have a dirty mind. A poignant expression on her face, the camera up close on the right side, as well as the sound guy, she's surrounded by feet and knees, the camera's rolling: *si iou on zi ozer saïde*, see you on the other side. Cut. She has to play up her accent, and her breathing, and how weak she is.

She had wanted to act with Desplechin, Carax, Noé, but not one of them contacted her; she remembers waiting after a so-called casting session when in fact the decisions had already been made. Now she's the one who gets to say the titles of the big Hollywood blockbusters and she's paid fifty thousand dollars for two days of shooting and they can get fucked. A twitch of impatience in Damon's fingers; she refocuses. There are women who think Damon is good-looking. She thinks he's white. *See you on the other side.* She warbles the words, with rising intonation, like a question: that's the one, the director loves it.

*

Olga wipes off her make-up, they're whacked. Natsumi and the make-up artist have already left. Two messages on her phone: a kiss from George, and a hi from Lloyd, asking if everything went well. That's kind of him.

Olga massages cleanser gel into her face. Mirror. Night falls.

'I've met someone.'

'How nice,' says Olga.

At first they trade clichés, stiff and rubbery like hamburger cheese. Then things thaw a little. Her make-up is running under the white gel, her eyes shiny with tears through the diluted mascara.

'He hasn't called me,' her red mouth utters.

'Since when?' asks Olga, wiping her face again with cotton wool.

'Two days.'

Olga smiles. 'Two days is nothing. Men, men…'

'But that's not the point.' She struggles under the cotton wool, turns to face Olga, rather than her own reflection. 'Something *really* did happen,'—she tries to think of the word—'a connection.'

All those words he said to her. She doesn't summon them; she lets them hover between Olga and her. Words like jelly, quivering and translucent, through which Olga recognises the two of them, her and him. Observes them, caught in the amber of the words, in the golden light of the evening. Sees them caught in love.

No, she's left something out.

'He is black.'

Olga doesn't understand.

'He is a black man,' she repeats. Why does she need to point that out? What has it got to do with the story? What kind of hair-splitting is she getting mixed up in? Why is she mixed up in it at all? That aching all through her body, in her throat, that weariness. Olga backs away. She recalls how Kouhouesso put some distance between her and him, not much, but measurable. That's it: it's exactly the same distance that Olga instinctively took, a tangible distance. It goes from here to there in space, in longitude and latitude, and it can be calculated by coordinates. Compared to the ocean or even to California, it doesn't make much sense, but relative to the human body, it can be understood as the measurement from white to black, the measurement of the prejudices with which, for two days, she's been battling.

Olga is Asian. It's blindingly obvious. Her eyes, her hair. A good example of the nomadic Hun tribe. From that part of Asia where the names end in -stan, from that huge interior below the Ural River where they still believe in Europe but where there are deserts and actual camels. Why didn't she choose a different confidante, someone like Natsumi? No. Natsumi is *yellow*, too. She has very pale skin, but she is not white, she is Japanese, *of Japanese origin* as they say in France; she's probably whiter than a Chinese person and much whiter than an Arab, but less white than a Spaniard and even less so than a Portuguese person.

Olga stares at Solange, and at her reflection, one after the other. The cleanser gel has melted and Solange looks naked, transparent. She feels as if Olga can sense her thoughts—which are arising from some mysterious place, from the murky depths of her village, far from Los Angeles, but lying low in the back of her head. She would like to apologise, tell Olga that we are all the same. She would like to open up her skin to show her universal Benetton colour.

Olga smiles but seems to hesitate before speaking. Even now, at this time of evening, sharing a bottle of Merlot in the dressing room, when everyone has left, Solange is her superior. Solange is the one on the screen, it's big budget, she's the Warner Bros girl, she's the one who ends up with bruises from the star. Olga purses her lips, half-disapproving, half-malicious. She laughs, her hand over her mouth. 'Did he have a big one?'

IN THE GOLDEN NOCTURNAL LIGHT

She wasn't asleep. It didn't feel like it. Or else she was in a dream that, on waking, left her with the image of a rational world.

The phone rings and she knows it's him.

'Hey.'

It's him.

There's a splintering in her chest and she wonders if he's saying *hey* because he's forgotten her name. 'Hey,' she says in turn.

Trying not to shriek. So he wrote down her number. He didn't take the Post-it note on the coffee pot, but he wrote down her number. Looked for some paper and a pencil, made the effort. No, she's stupid, he must have put it straight into his phone.

He asks if he's disturbing her. It's not exactly polite small talk, at two in the morning. Questions, answers, possible strategies and responses—who cares: her chest is bursting with joy. 'No, it's fine.' Her voice is husky.

'Can I come by?'

'Yes.'

There you go. That's it. He hung up. She drank a glass of water.

Still today she rubs the recollection against her memory and it produces heat, redness. Flashes of joy. Once again, she can see herself, feel herself entering the waiting state, as if entering an effervescent sea. Blissfully waiting for him.

If he is coming from Topanga, she has almost an hour ahead of her. She must have slept a bit: in the mirror she has sleep residue on her eyelids and mouth. She brushes her hair but leaves it a bit messy. No make-up. 'Straight out of bed.' She's naked under her dressing-gown. Too much. She puts on one of her French camisoles. She has a collection of them, simple, cotton—American women don't realise how sexy camisoles are. But he is not American. What is a sexy woman for him? Jeans and a sweater, no shirt? The I-was-just-reading-quietly look. After all, she's at home.

She boils the kettle. No, better to open some wine. The Saint-Émilion her father sent her last Christmas. She puts on a dab of perfume, wonders whether to take a shower. Did she perspire a bit during the phone call? But there are men who like body odour. In fact, she does, too. Music.

The music she would have put on this evening if, instead of going to bed, she had been reading in the living room in her at-home outfit. What would he like? What woman listening to what music would he like?

No, he can take her as she is, dressing-gown and camisole. At two in the morning. She hesitates. Don't light the candle. The situation couldn't be clearer: no need to overdo it. Don't wear a bra. A woman at home doesn't wear a bra. Unless extreme measures are required. Her breasts are like those of a Japanese girl; she hopes he doesn't mind. Kouhouesso. Really, what sort of a name is that. Kouhouesso Nwokam.

She's so happy. So happy she'll get to see him. He's going to come. The certainty of it.

She's ready.

She rearranges her bouquet of peonies, cuts the stems a little, changes the water. Cleans the coffee table while she's at it.

She lies on the couch. She's hot. He should be here by now. She gets up. Grabs her book. Lies down again. She tries to read. Perhaps he changed his mind. That would be terrible. Perhaps he was held up somewhere. Or gave up, because it was so late?

She sends him a text. No answer. She nods off briefly. Later, she knows she's arrived at the edge of a cliff. At the tip of the waiting. The tip is embedded in her chest. She feels it, reddened by the flames. The edge of the cliff is a narrow wire, a metal blade. She is burning up. It's almost four o'clock. She picks up her phone again, he definitely called, she didn't dream it, it's there on the screen. That short conversation. She puts his number into her contacts. Kouhouesso. Kouhouesso Nwokam.

It's early afternoon in France. She would be out walking. In the streets of Paris. In the freedom of the streets of Paris. A simple little skirt and heels. No ties to anything, daydreaming. Right now in France, Rose is at work. Text to Rose. Reply: call later on Skype. But the buzz of her phone already makes her feel better. In her apartment perched at the top of Bel Air, she has not disappeared. She has not disintegrated somewhere between Europe and America. At the juncture of the two continents. Separated by two fault lines, one that slices through the Atlantic, the other that will one day sever California from the rest of the world.

Kouhouesso. Kouhouesso. Nwokam. Up until now she had scarcely thought about Africa, other than to send off a cheque. Africa and its starving children. Africa and its machete massacres. Africa, where her father was born, although he never talks about it. The huge foreign land, a drop of liquid, hanging below Europe: never been on her itinerary. She worked in a pub in Moscow. Earned twenty thousand dollars for a one-hour performance in Hong Kong. Received a prize for *Musette* in Japan. From east to west and from west to east, but never south.

She turns on her computer, does a satellite search of

Africa. Cameroon is at the bottom of a right angle, one of many countries. The English-speaking part isn't marked. A band of mist follows the coastline, Nigeria, Benin, Togo, Ghana, Ivory Coast, Liberia, a string of lagoons and towns with names like Togo, Tegbi, Yemorasa, Akwidaa, Sassandra. When you get to Cape Palmas you end up in the ocean. If you head in the other direction, straight east, you find vegetation. You arrive in the Congo. Which extends a long way south. There are wide rivers with oval islands floating like leaves fallen from the trees. She learns that there are two Congos. The app can't decide where to mark the border between Kinshasa Congo and Brazzaville Congo. The two cities, K and B, are opposite each other on the two sides of the river, but further away each riverbank is marked by a red line indicating conflict. It's as if the islands were floating without a country, as if the river slipped stateless between its banks. Wide, but no wider (she turns the Earth around with her finger) than the Gironde and its mouth, where from Médoc you can see the lights of Royan, in the distance, through the grey.

Rose's face appears at the top of the screen, *bilibili*. Rose is in her office at the Medical Psychology Centre on Boulevard Ornano in Paris. She mustn't have had time to have lunch. While Solange is in her camisole on the slopes of Bel Air. Day and night at the same time. You never get used to it, that's for sure. Rose looks at her: 'Wow, you look beautiful.' Solange looks at Rose, her best friend for twenty years. Tries telepathically to transmit what she'd like to say. Kouhouesso Nwokam. She wonders if it's operating between them, what Rose calls transference. Rose describes it as a continuous transmission of radio waves between shrink and patient, in both directions, wherever you are on the planet.

Kouhouesso Nwokam. Kouhouesso Nwokam telepathically. Probably a bit tricky. Was he going to come, after all? The screen image wobbles and there are crackling sounds, sandstorms are gusting, enormous cables have been cast into the ocean so that Solange can speak to her friend Rose.

'What do you think—I'm speaking to you as shrink—a man sleeps with you and seems to have a good time, but then doesn't call you, and then, when he does call, he makes you wait again?'

'What time is it?' asks Rose, and it's not clear if she's worried about her friend or her next patient.

'Four o'clock.'

Four o'clock on her side of the globe. In the morning. The sky is mauve-blue over Bel Air.

On the other side of Earth, Rose looks up at her pale sky. Solange hurries on. 'This time it's different. What I feel—even allowing for the fact that he might not feel it—is special, precious, it hasn't happened to me for a long time, perhaps since we were adolescents, although'—she silences her straight away—'I don't want to go back there.'

Rose says, 'Waiting is an illness. A mental illness. Often a female one.'

Solange says, 'What I feel means so much to me that I'm fine to wait, I'm fine to wait a bit. Waiting isn't even that bad. And, you know, he's not like the others, the others you're thinking about, it's not a repeat performance.'

She doesn't feel like telling her that he's black. Nor that she's only known him for three days. Various ideas are running through her mind. Various details. On a couch, she wouldn't know where to begin.

A sudden image pops up: Saint Teresa made into a Bernini statue, spotlit by myriad beams, each one sharp but exquisite, each one leading her back to him. Which beam does she follow first? Which does she extend further? Rose wouldn't understand. At worst, she'd pronounce some platitude. Even shock would be hurtful. So he was black, surely there was no need to kick up a huge fuss about it? In the village where they were born, everyone was white, except—now that she thinks about it—Monsieur Kudeshayan, the grocer. Who was not exactly black: his skin was darker than Kouhouesso's, charcoal-grey, grey like lead, but he was from Pakistan or somewhere around there. You don't call those black people black. Oddly enough.

Perhaps something cropped up. But he could have called her. Perhaps he fell asleep. Surely he didn't have an accident? Another of those ideas that pop into her mind: do black people have a tendency to be late? Do Africans have a slightly idiosyncratic relationship with time? The beam pierces her. Is that a racist thought? Is she being bombarded by racist beams? Is Kouhouesso black in the sense of—is Kouhouesso the black people? So she would be the Basque people?

She would like to talk about this with someone. She would like to talk about this with him. She would like to go to the nightclub with him. Basque, on the corner of Vine and Hollywood. She would like to speak to him about where she comes from.

And how about with women? Don't they have a slightly idiosyncratic relationship with women?

Those beams, they're flashes of lightning. Could Rose possibly accuse her—let's say, simply put her attraction down to the undeniable fact that he has dark skin, and, as well, an impossible name, African in any case—could Rose reduce her crazy desire for this undreamt-of man to the stupid stubborn fact that he is black?

*

The doorbell. It's him.

The precise object of her waiting—him, *here*. Him and not another. The waiting had been so immense that he had been, as it were, dissolved by it. He had become—him, this man—inconceivable. A constellation whose existence is known, visible in the sky, but beyond reach and consequently abstract, and in the end irrelevant.

She had the strange impression of possibly being content with something else, with someone else, another man or even a film she might have chosen. What would the film have been about? And what other man—would he have been *black*? The annoying question appeared to her as if in a dream, involuntarily. An angry crowd was yelling at her, fists raised beneath the windows in her mind. A mechanical crowd, with huge keys in their backs.

Him. He was *here*. Did he want a coffee, some water, some wine? He chose wine. Or an orange juice? She had very good oranges. She was talking rubbish. Her pulse was pounding in her throat. She was not used to it. *Him*. He helped himself to wine. Didn't mention being late—was he in fact *late*? In the end, had he actually mentioned a time? He was sitting there, at ease, his magnetic field spread around him like a cape, and she no longer knew why she had expended so much energy waiting for him; why she had not simply waited for him, like you wait for someone who is coming, someone who is going to ring the bell and sit down with his glass, his ease, and his psychedelic coat.

She was hungry. Another image superimposed itself, an absurd image, on the TV one day, of a tall, thin Ethiopian woman leaning against a tree, eating the bark. She had no image in her mind for English-speaking Cameroon.

He was speaking to her. She was not listening. She got up to find some pistachios. She had waited for him so long that she was still waiting for him. The waiting kept cruising under its own momentum, like a boat. She was in the boat. And he was, too, sitting on his couch in the middle of the sea, floating, glass in hand, and only in a distracted and enchanting way paying attention to the passing cruise ship packed with passengers talking furiously.

Am I in love with him? Was that love, the way she waited and now, without listening, watched his beautiful lips move over his beautiful teeth? She wanted to kiss him. He was speaking animatedly, with passion, his voice mellow and soft, deep and throaty. As if his initial deep silence now resonated in his words.

Then she realised he was drunk. Like the first time. But she wasn't: she had no way of knowing precisely what was making him so impassioned. She was the slow-motion spectator of a speeded-up film. Or perhaps she was just tired.

She looked at this man, his magnetism, sitting in her home at four o'clock in the morning and she wondered if that was it, what she wanted. She wanted him to kiss her. All men want to kiss her. The shy ones drink first, then it's as per normal. A normal man would kiss her. Even her less attractive girlfriends, her girlfriends who aren't actresses, tell her what men are like and they're like that. Especially at an indecent hour in the home of a woman in a camisole to whom you've already said intoxicating words.

BRASS LEGGINGS

He talked to her about the Congo. Not any old Congo, not the little Brazzaville Congo, no, the big Kinshasa one, where very quickly the road runs out and there are just the long arms of the river, which she had looked at on Google Earth three hours earlier. The coincidence was disturbing. She was going to chat about the islands—but he had drawn breath to introduce a new topic of conversation, and was now talking about *Heart of Darkness*. He told her about Conrad's novel. The story of a man who is looking for a man. Marlow looking for Kurtz, a retired officer from a colonial regiment, a 'devil of a rapacious and pitiless folly'. Conrad's Congo is 'something great and invincible, like evil or truth'. And Europe—white-faced Europe, the premonition of genocides. He cited the African woman in the novel 'with a slight jingle and flash of barbarous ornaments', 'brass leggings to the knees' (she pictured the sorceress in *Kirikou*). He cited the 'Intended', 'this pale visage', blonde and diaphanous (she pictured herself). Was it a racist novel? No. But it was time for an African to seize power in Hollywood. It was time to take back from America the history of indigenous people.

She was overwhelmed with tiredness. Couldn't they just have a *normal* conversation? But he kept talking: he wanted to make a film adaptation of *Heart of Darkness*, something different from Coppola's *Apocalypse Now* and, in any case, *on location*—a crazy project, he was aware of that, his first film as a director and with equatorial ambitions to transport a crew into the heart of the forest and, once there, attempt to mount that masterpiece of a novel. Coppola went to the Philippines in order to film Vietnam; he would go to the Congo to film the Congo.

She interrupted him. She hadn't read the novel, but wasn't it a bit of a cliché: *Heart of Darkness*? A bit too run-of-the-mill for Africa? He protested. What he was interested in was precisely the stereotype, the ultimate cliché, what white people saw when they thought about Africa: darkness and elephants.

Was she white people? That beam pierced her chest. Did he see her as a white person? Was he—worse—here *because* she was white? She had been loved for her buttocks, for her talent, for her celebrity, but never for her colour. Or else all men, all the white people who had desired her up until now, had only done it *on condition* that she was white?

She turned away and was startled by their reflection. In the bay window against the night sky, a man and a woman leaning into each other. She was struck by their beauty. The curve of the woman and the straight line of the man, her lying down, him sitting up, classically beautiful, thin and so Hollywood, her face-on and him in profile, yin-yang, snap: both perfectly matched. He could have any woman of any colour. She could have any man she wanted. Everyone on Earth may have wanted to sleep with him, but he was here with her.

She moved closer to him. He kept talking. His strange gaze fixed on her, on the surface of her camisole, as if he were carrying out a topographical survey. Surprisingly and almost inadvertently, the Congo had allowed itself to be enslaved. Belgium was a tick on a giant's back, and how do you even locate the tick when humans, since childhood, have stared at the immense green patch that is the centre of Africa? He was describing, with circular gestures, how shot after shot, *mise en abyme* after *mise en abyme,* his film would become more and more claustrophobic, 'burrowing deep into the centre of the Earth'. And suddenly she had the faint hope that someone might know, finally know—perhaps him—where the centre of the world was. Everywhere, and in men, she had searched for it, that centre, that intensity. From the sound of him, it was over there, deep in the Congo. With him.

He was impetuous, bitter and wise. She wanted to taste that charm; she wanted him to be quiet but to keep talking to her; she wanted to devour his mouth. In France, when a man spends a long time explaining something to a woman, it's above all in order to sleep with her. She opened another bottle. She hadn't considered matching her nail polish with her camisole, deep pink on flesh pink—and, what does it even mean: flesh-pink white?

'To be honest,' she began, 'I'd completely forgotten, for instance, that Belgium had invaded the Congo.'

'Not invaded. Colonised, violated, carved up, butchered. Fifteen million dead. And France. Twenty thousand dead for the only railway from the Congo to the ocean.'

'As many as that.' She sighed. Her living room was filled with skulls.

He checked his phone—she was frightened it was a text from another woman—but he started to read the first page of Conrad's novel out loud to her from his screen: a gloomy London, the Thames, a ship in the night. He envisaged a murky opening shot, black sky, and then the sea emerging in a fade-in.

'And you'll find producers here, in Hollywood?'

He paused, an actor's pause.

'You know who will play Kurtz?'

A new beam illuminated her. She understood.

'George.'

'And who do you think will play the Intended?'

A rush of blood, her lips went taut, she felt the urge to inflate them and raise herself, yes her, towards him, towards the sky, towards an outlandish future, an expedition to the Congo, a marvellous and terrifying film shoot.

'Gwyneth Paltrow.'

She got up. There are always moments of huge disappointment in the life of an actress, dishonesty, rigged horse-trading, nocturnal betrayals, and boorish behaviour. One of her nails was torn. She felt a childish regret, the silly idea that, if she had matched her nails to her outfit, he would have given her the role.

He explained the finances of the project, the money George was putting in, and perhaps Studio Canal, and a producer in Lagos, even Africana Studies at UCLA. Why did she feel like crying at this point? She still fancied his lips, that's what was so exasperating: her raging desire. His project would never get off the ground. George was forever having those philanthropic notions, and anyway that would be the biggest bit of miscasting of his career—George as a bad guy? But there was always the challenge, for a star like him, to surpass Brando. Even in a shambolic production in the depths of the jungle.

And it wouldn't be a shambolic production. With George on board it would end up on screens all over the world. The perfect UFO. A huge action movie, but also a bit arty. A big deal in any case, entrusted to an African, with the anything-but-vulgar touch that George adds to Hollywood, and that this man Kouhouesso also has, *yeah, baby, he's got it.*

Gwyneth Paltrow? That pathetic beanpole?

She placed her lips on his. It was like kissing a bouquet of peonies. Fleshy, luscious and beaded with freshness. Peonies saturated with a strong liqueur, soft, manly flowers, intoxicating.

She could no longer see his face, nor his roaming eyes. Their outlines cancelled each other out, cyclopean heat and moist mouths. He kept talking, but less. It was as if his mouth was blossoming from his scratchy cheeks, his lips even sweeter, and she was melting, soft and hard and tender and tense. He pulled away for a second and she thought he was going to preach to her again about the Congo, but no. He was staring at her. He looked happy.

Lying next to his big body, her camisole slipped above her head, she was once again touching this man, who was speaking to her about herself, who was saying wonderful things, who was burying himself in her and then pulling back as if reluctantly. She clung to him, until their bodies blurred in the embrace, deep, but not effusive. It was easy, so easy to remain in this marvellous suspension of breath where she was no longer waiting for him—it was he who was waiting for her.

Later, her thigh was resting on his thigh, and her arm was on his arm, and she was so white and he was so black that it made her laugh, it was tantalising, appetising, almost like a pastry confection; their bodies were so distinct one from the other, touched each other so unequivocally, ended and began exactly at the demarcation of the skins, and they wanted to start again just for that, to check once again that here is me and there is you and that we can locate ourselves and take pleasure in that, precisely that, the decorative difference, invented especially to look good. And he laughed to see her laugh and she said to herself, *if he laughs he loves me*. If he laughs we will keep on laughing and taking our pleasure.

The crows were cawing on the electricity wires; the sky was a milky blue. Their reflection had disappeared into the bay window. There was nothing left of them but their real bodies; there was nothing left of them but the two of them. The image of them had retreated to where images reside, in the folds of the Hollywood hills, in the shadows.

PART II

AND YOU GHOSTS RISE BLUE
FROM ALCHEMY

The light woke her, and the sensation of lying with him. She never slept for long. She breathed in the divine smell of his hair. The incense from his cathedral of hair. From his *dreadlocks*. She let them envelop her, wrap around her. They were a bit itchy, the ends prickled, they rolled like beads in the bed. That's what left the marks in the morning, etched into her skin. During the day she watched these marks slowly fade, like secret wedding rings, around her arms, her shoulders, her waist.

Close to his head it was soft and fluffy. No, they weren't braids. They were delicate coils. She looked at him, this astounding specimen, caught in the sheets of her bed. It sometimes seemed to her as if a creature with tentacles was gripping her from all sides. She didn't dare move, for fear of waking him.

Gently, she reached for a book. 'And you ghosts rise blue from alchemy…' Years of school and teachers, in Clèves and then in Bordeaux, and she hadn't read Césaire, she hadn't read Senghor, let alone Achebe or Soyinka. She'd never even heard of the last two. He'd had to spell them out to her. She'd felt illiterate. And she didn't know Fanon—and she was French? Nor Tchicaya U Tam'si, from the Congo? Nor Sony Labou Tansi, from the other Congo? Or even Tsitsi Dangarembga, from Zimbabwe? Or Bessie Head, from Botswana? (Where the hell was Botswana?) What she couldn't find in French she read in English. She read lying next to him, in silence, for hours. She was looking for answers. She was looking for the book that would tell their story. That would tell her the future. She tried to read from his perspective, to become the thing that he had loved, here, right here. Was it that female character? He slept in. He went to sleep late.

She had eventually hidden the photo of her son. She had given it some thought. In the photo he was only five; he certainly didn't make her seem old. One day, of course, she'd talk about it with him. They'd get round to it. But all that time before—the village, Bordeaux, Paris and even Los Angeles—it was as if, before him, there was nothing. As if time began with the mornings lying against him. What had she done during all those years? Before this intensity?

There were other photos, of Rose and her, and of her brother, in black and white, but—even assuming he had noticed them—he didn't ask questions. She looked at her son in the photo, with his face from another place, from another time. The time when the bike had training wheels. Where was she? In Paris. The time, oddly enough, of that other lover, Brice. She only remembered it now—not Brice, but the fact that he was black. Brice's colour had been of no importance at all. Was it, stupidly, because he was not very dark? Or because, like her, he was French? His West Indian accent, his family from the islands, it was—anecdotal, cosmetic. She didn't care in the slightest. They spent their time in nightclubs blowing money from the commercials they did during those years. They danced. He was good-looking, twenty, peroxide hair very short. He was only interested in auditions. For the agencies, black was fashionable: night-time, Thierry Mugler, Nick Cave, Tim Burton, the last echoes of the New Wave. An airy, twirling memory, like a dress. And perhaps, in his own way, he was not black. She remembered in particular that he liked boys. Girls, too, but also boys. When he left her, she was not unhappy, but she lost weight. In haste and in terror, she had investigated his background. At that time, Haitians, heroin addicts and homosexuals were the only ones rumoured to have AIDS. For her, Haiti and the West Indies were one and the same.

No AIDS. She forgot him. And she forgot that she had had at least one black lover after all. Brice was colourless, like her at the time. Their pigmentary difference was no big deal.

Kouhouesso woke up. Said *hey*, still in a slightly surprised tone. Rubbed his eyes with the flat of his hands. Got up to piss. She stayed there, her heart pounding. He came back. Wrapped her in his arms. Settled himself, taking his time, magnificently. They made love. Occasionally they laughed. Even then, she did not know what was going on. She only knew what was in her mind: that she was at the centre of the world, in his shoulders, his arms, his hair.

She had to keep him a bit longer. But, between the moment he opened his eyes and when he left, it was always the same scenario, the minutes flew by and then he was standing up. He put on his clothes from the day before, and left. Never showered at her place. Didn't call her. But if she sent him a text—'Miss you', 'I'm thinking about you'—he replied, just a few words—'me too' or 'lots of love'.

Lots of love, that's the way her English pen pal had signed off her letters, when they were fifteen.

*

Out of pride, she made herself put him to the test with her own silence. Two days, three days…ten days. She ended up capitulating and sent a text proposing a date. He was always up for it. With astounding candour, he asked why she hadn't been in touch. And he was punctual, ever since she had rebuked him, in savage French, for being late the first time.

He had raised his voice a little: '*Nous n'avions pas précisé une heure.*'

He hardly ever responded in French. Where he came from, they spoke English and French and numerous (three hundred!) other languages. *Nous n'avions pas précisé une heure*: the sentence was a bit odd, but mostly it was his accent that was odd. An accent like the comedian Michel Leeb's. For a second, she thought he was making fun of her. That he was overdoing it. In her village, in Clèves, in the eighties, there was always someone imitating Michel Leeb imitating black people. If he had said in English, just as firmly, *we didn't say what time*, she might have been intimidated. But she wanted to smile now. When he said it, *précisé* became a warble, with a rolling 'r', the first syllable emphasised, and three big open vowels. As for 'time', it was a throaty sound, sombre and menacing. She remembered the ugly old ebony masks brought back from Senegal by her paternal grandparents, well before she was born, and laid out on a Basque tablecloth. She had never thought twice about any of it.

Afterwards she forgot. Something took over, kept taking over. She had read *Heart of Darkness*. Enough of it to know that his project was madness. Short of digitising the forest, renting a green-key studio and dumping the actors into the jungle? Marlow didn't meet the Intended until the end. It was a beautiful scene—if short and cruel, the Intended waiting for Kurtz in vain—but you could get a few wonderful shots (mourning dress, her hair in an ash-blonde bun, 'not very young': in Hollywood terms, exactly her age). 'Her fair hair seemed to catch all the remaining light in a glimmer of gold.' You could even imagine inserting scenes where Kurtz dreamed about her, scenes where she appeared, diaphanous in the jungle—after all, it was a novel teeming with visions, a hallucinatory novel, miasmic, mystical. 'I am proud to know I understand him better than anyone on earth…' Yes, it was a role for her. Yes, Kurtz dreamed about the Intended and she, Solange, would go into the jungle. Or into the studio, but with Kouhouesso.

*

On Skype, Rose told her that it was a bad sign when a man never invited you to his place. What was he hiding? Another woman? Several other women? Seven women with their throats cut? Dirty socks? A mess? Solange still hadn't mentioned the colour of Kouhouesso's skin, or his name, but it seemed as if the telepathic waves were being transmitted through the network.

He shared his place with another tenant, Jessie. Who was never there. And who paid most of the rent. A villa that was almost as beautiful as George's. Kouhouesso was on the top floor, with a terrace that overlooked the canyon. The first time he took her there, she couldn't stop walking around. A huge light-filled loft, books everywhere, as well as a few accent pieces of furniture. A big bed, a large beige rug. Computers resting directly on the floor, lots of technology.

She wandered around barefoot on the wooden floor, euphoric. She wore a simple white cotton dress, with thin crocheted straps. On the wall there was a—what was it?—giant painted skin, parchment, a sort of frieze with angels and swords, a weird alphabet. And lying casually on the ground was a huge head with a serene expression, a black female torso made out of yellow material. She was so beautiful, this woman whose face was lined with stripes, that it made her feel weary, perhaps from jealousy. 'Where did you buy it?' She imagined him negotiating the price of this prodigious object in some village market. He had bought it in the British Museum gift shop. A copy, of course. 'Who is it?' He burst out laughing. Do you ask 'who is it?' about the Venus de Milo? It was the King of Ife. Not a woman but a king. The most famous head in African art, along with the Fang masks, perhaps. As for the scroll on the wall, it was an Ethiopian magic scroll, to conjure the devil in Amharic.

She thought he said America and took on a knowing look.

The sun was setting over the canyon; they were listening to Leonard Cohen. He opened a bottle that she'd brought, his Chinese eyes became two slits and a trace of something tender was hovering around his face, near his eyelids, near his mouth, an apparition, like a hummingbird, something swift and nebulous. Perhaps that was what held her back, what she couldn't quite…the fleeting gentleness in a mask. She wanted to kiss him where the soft folds opened up, here, there, and him hidden beneath. 'Terrified by love,' Rose would say.

He was going to see Leonard Cohen in concert soon. Did she know that the famous singer's main adversary was not the Vietnam war or the American right wing, but his own depression? He wondered what role the holocaust of the Jews (he didn't say 'the Shoah') played in this lifelong depression.

As for her, she wondered when the concert was and why he didn't invite her.

*

When she woke, the loft was empty. 'Kouhouesso?' She had only ever said his name in a hushed voice, in his arms. She had never said it to anyone else. She hadn't even spoken to George about him. It was strange saying his name, *Kouhouesso*, out loud, in the silence. Like blasphemy. Sounds that she didn't know how to say in any language, intonations into empty space, of an imaginary Africa, magic and formidable.

Jessie was there. They were both smoking by the pool. They had opened some beers and were talking about the *Heart of Darkness* project. Jessie (she guessed as soon as she saw the villa) was the famous Jessie, the film star, one of the rare black Hollywood superstars. Less famous than George, but still…She reached her hand out to him. Jessie shot a few salacious glances at his buddy. She smiled, modest. Intimidated, not by this guy, but by Kouhouesso's silence.

He was looking away. Was he annoyed at being seen with her? Or with a *white woman*? She swatted the idea like a fly. Jessie offered her some green tea: 'All girls drink green tea.' She went for the green tea. A Mexican housemaid appeared; she hadn't come across her the day before. 'I said to Kou,' he continued, 'never date a French girl. The last time I dated a French girl, there was a slight disagreement. *Petite chérie* was driving down the canyon at full speed—never argue with a woman at the wheel—I told her, slow down, you're going to kill us. She peels off into the side road and *bang!* There goes my Maybach.'

He was not speaking to her or to Kouhouesso, but to the canyon, so it seemed. From what he was saying, Maybach was a make of car. She guessed it from the context, as she did with a lot of things.

'I want to get out. She backs up. And *bang*, again. There goes the the back left bumper!'

Kouhouesso was laughing; he had obviously heard the story before. It was a shrill laugh, a bit impatient. She tried to catch his eye. To discern any criticism, but he had put on his mask. And they had gone back to talking about the film. Things were more advanced than she had imagined.

She got the impression that it was time for her to go, leave them—to work.

BEL AIR

The waiting began again, waiting as a chronic disease. A sticky fever, a torpor. And, between the times she saw him, the reinfections, she slowly immersed herself in the paradox that she was waiting for a man she was losing sight of, an invented man. The waiting was the reality; her waiting was the proof of his life, as if the body of this man, when she held him in her arms, was made of the texture of time, fatally fleeting.

It was twelve days later, through what seemed a coincidence to her, that she learned of the date of the Leonard Cohen concert. Because exactly twelve days later she received a text: 'Amazing concert. Wish you were here.'

She saw on the internet that Leonard Cohen was playing, right then, at the Nokia Theatre. She couldn't care less about Leonard Cohen: she had pinpointed him, Kouhouesso, *here*, like those arrows on street maps. *Wish you were here*—the fury and the frustration (all he had to do was invite her, get organised, plan!)—and then another beep, a second message: '*Je ne t'oublie guère.*'

Je ne t'oublie guère.

Twelve days, not a word, and now 'I can scarcely stop thinking about you.' Only an African could write such quaint French, so charming—she understood (knowing him, yes, knowing him better and better) that he wasn't the slightest bit interested in her feelings for him. In English he treated her as an equal. As one foreigner to another foreigner. In America. On American territory.

Suzanne takes you down...

She let Leonard Cohen's song ripple through her mind. Replacing *Suzanne* with *Solange*. Sorrowfully. Later, in the middle of the night, by dint of humming (if she hummed enough, he would return), he returned. She did not chastise him at all. They opened a bottle; he had already drunk a lot. An *amazing* concert—his friends loved it. So he might have been ready, as well, to introduce her to his friends?

'I never know when we're going to see each other again.'

'But I'm here.'

Every exchange in French was a victory. Proof, even, of his love for her. She had lured him onto her turf. He couldn't stop thinking about her. In French.

'Twelve days without even a text message.'

'Twelve days?'

He didn't believe her. He was truly sorry. 'I've been really busy.'

She was in between jobs, and he, apparently, wasn't looking anymore. He said he'd become an actor by chance, just to pay the rent. What he cared about was making his film. He was in 'pre-production'. She cancelled her girlfriends, her personal trainer, her yoga, her shrink, in order to be available for him. He appeared, then disappeared. He was a man who existed intermittently. When he left—she saw him disappear in his car, then saw his car disappear behind Hotel Bel-Air—he dematerialised. A phantom. She held empty space in her arms, clutched nothingness. Away from her, his existence was like an impossible memory.

They made love. He touched her and, all of a sudden, she was overcome again, transformed. He was busy, *très occupé*: she no longer heard his rolling 'r's, she only heard the turbulence of what she didn't know. The emptiness of her own days. The frenzy of missing him.

He went into the bathroom. Then downstairs to the living room. She could hear him talking on the phone. Typing on a keyboard. She wondered what he was up to, all those hours, instead of being in bed next to her.

She joined him. He looked up from his computer. She said the first thing that popped into her head: 'I'd really like to go to Africa.'

'No, you wouldn't,' he replied, returning to the computer.

'Yes,' she insisted, like a child. 'I'd like to see'—she stopped herself from saying 'the elephants'—'the Victoria Falls, and the source of the Nile.'

He shut his computer. '*Africa*, as such, does not exist.'

He was so cool, the way he said amazing things like that. But she had a good memory, at least short-term, and felt a rising panic.

'You said it yourself, the other evening, *Africa*, as such. The first night at my place, when you arrived so late. Yes, you did. You said *the green patch which constitutes the centre of Africa*. It was nice.'

He started laughing his weirdly shrill laugh, as if he'd borrowed it from another body.

'Africa is an ethnological fiction. There are *many* Africas. Same thing for the colour black: it's an invention. Africans are not black, they are Bantu and Baka, Nilote and Mandinka, Khoikhoi and Swahili.'

Those syllables were so foreign to her that she couldn't manage to pick them out in the sentence. They sounded like one long word to her. And when she was to say to him later, 'Africa is an ethnological fiction', he would once again come out with that weird laugh, his eyes blank, and that calm, almost weary, suppressed anger. Where did she get the idea that Africa didn't exist? She was as unlikely to risk saying 'from you' as she was to say 'I love you'.

Her brain tended to lose traction when she was with him. She didn't have a single comeback. She knew nothing.

71

She hadn't read a single book. She no longer knew how to read. As for him, this man she loved, about whom she was learning so much, his tastes, his past, his pleasures, his strength, his talent and lack of humour, whose moods she was beginning to dread, she knew nothing about him.

By means of a phenomenon to do with time and space, with history and locations, with violence, a phenomenon that had nothing magical about it but which she could see was distorting the space between them, the sentences he uttered turned into other sentences in her mouth. Word for word, the same sentences took on a meaning that she didn't want. An atrocious meaning. This unmagical phenomenon was making her wait for a man whose ancestors had been slaughtered and enslaved by her own ancestors. Exploitation and slaughter continued, so it seemed, yes, continued with the consent of some of *her people*, but without *her people* ever relinquishing their dominant status.

He didn't utter these complicated truths the way she did. He mocked her *lefty blinkered idealism*. He agreed that *Africa* was in a desperate state, that he had turned his back on his native land, but he simply wanted to try to tell a story without getting waylaid carrying on about sacks of rice.

And when she maintained that the rice, sometimes, despite the despotic corruption and the big business of charities, still reached a few starving mouths, he outlined the path that rice took, from the rice field where it is better treated than the person who harvests it, to the mouth of the person who swallows it, each then separated by thousands of kilometres, by millions of containers then blocked at customs, by billions of dollars in arms and cheap rubbish: thousands and millions and billions which would not suffice to give any idea of the established, ongoing, calculated scale of the exploitation of human beings by human beings and of the planet by its *homo erectus* tenants.

She was born where she was born, into the skin that was her skin, surrounded by the words that surrounded her. She worked out that it wasn't exactly that white people don't have anything to say about black people (they never stopped, ever since she was a little girl they'd been going on about them); no, it was that white people don't have anything to say to black people about black people. They can't even repeat things.

At dawn, he would finally come to bed; they would make love again. He fell asleep straight away. And went out into the yellow afternoons, into the emptiness of the sun at its zenith.

HOLLYWOOD DOOWYLLOH

She wouldn't see him for ten days, then suddenly he'd turn up. Completely available for her. She started to think that he did exist after all, that he wouldn't walk out of her life just like that. In silence, she endured his interludes of silence. Put all her efforts into keeping quiet about her empty days—more heartbroken than empty.

They usually saw each other at her place. He liked the layout, upstairs, the living room; he could work at night without disturbing her; at Jessie's (that's how he referred to his place) the bed was in the middle of the loft. But at Jessie's, she argued, there was a pool, a really private pool, not like the one in her apartment block. She could go swimming naked. She liked that pool.

'Come on, it's lovely,' she said, splashing around, her two

small breasts like floats. 'A real little fish,' he said admiringly, before returning to the shade of the loft. She floated on her back, eyes open onto the Californian sun. Let herself be dazed by the glaring light and by the listless palms, in the blue oval of the world. She could stay there forever, him working inside, her floating outside, in a place of their own.

She started to dream about Christmas. She had planned to spend a few days in France; actually she already had her ticket, bought three months ahead of time, business class but a good deal. She didn't dare enquire about his plans. All at once, it seemed vulgar. Anyway, was it an important date for him? Was he even Catholic?

She gave him a spare key and introduced him to the concierge. The concierge laughed and said that they had already met, thanks. And an astounding thing happened: Kouhouesso said some outlandish syllables and the other guy responded with similar extravagant sounds, and she stood there, gaping, like a fish out of water.

It was *camfranglais*. 'How did you know you were from the same place?' (She said 'place' the way you'd point out, with your finger, a white spot on an explorer's map.) He laughed and replied that she, too, recognised her tribe, the many Basque people in Los Angeles. When he laughed like that, she lost heart. She was overcome by the particular weariness that seemed to be connected with their relationship.

He went away. Unmitigated waiting. Oh, she knew about waiting: waiting between films, between takes. But this waiting was different. She lived only for his approval. She waited for life to start up again.

She tried to remember what she had been like before, the way, when you're sick, you try to remember being healthy: a state of being that you take for granted. She had been ambitious; she had crossed the ocean. Her agent was one of the best; she had been in major films, bit parts, for sure, but major films nonetheless. She had a project with Floria, quite another thing from the role as the Intended. And Soderbergh was sniffing around. Yes, she had waited, she had believed in her talent, she had kept her figure and looked after her body. She remembered all the time she spent choosing vegetables at the health shop, making her own smoothies, and doing her yoga with her teacher. And what else? She probably read, she waited for the delivery of her lunch, calorie-calculated by her dietician, she took elocution lessons, she called friends. In the evening she tried on clothes, she went to screenings, to opening nights, to dinners, occasionally to TV screenings. Buying her Bel Air home had monopolised her time and she had to work a lot to keep up the mortgage repayments. And, during all that time, he was in the city. And she didn't know. What a surprise: she didn't miss him. Before meeting him, she was fine without him. She wasn't even aware of his magnetic field: she was completely, blissfully unaware of him.

From now on, the instant his car drove behind the Hotel Bel-Air, she stayed at the bay window as if a fish bowl had dropped on top of her. She fluttered around, gasping for air. The instant at the bay window was the beginning of emptiness, if emptiness is the form of a distraught urge, wanting so much to follow him and banging into the glass. On the other side: life.

After two days, she reached rock bottom, under a white, clinical light. It couldn't have been clearer. She called; he didn't pick up. She was familiar with the humiliation of texting without a response. Yes, he replied. He always ended up replying, but so long afterwards that it was not a reply: it was an event, a surprise, the sensational return of the hero.

*

One day he booked two tickets for the Cindy Sherman exhibition at MOCA. So he liked contemporary art? Cindy Sherman made up as a clown, Cindy Sherman disguised as a witch—she remembered that at her place, in the study, he had left a small poster of Cindy Sherman. He must have wanted to please her.

'What a fabulous actress,' he said. She was annoyed. Until now, he had not watched any of her films, except the first one. He had arrived one evening bursting with questions: how had Godard directed her? Did Godard give you the script beforehand? Did Godard make you redo scenes? Godard, Godard: she was eighteen when she'd acted for Jean-Luc; she didn't have a clue who the guy with the Swiss accent was. 'He was always ducking off to play tennis.'

Kouhouesso burst out laughing.

Did he think she was good, at least? Did he think she was *so much* younger?

At what pace did he want to go round the exhibition? Would he prefer to talk or stay quiet? Be alone, or share his impressions? Cindy Sherman in despair next to a telephone. Cindy Sherman as obese depressive. Cindy Sherman as granny with doggy. Cindy Sherman as blue-stained corpse. The dreadful impression of seeing her future unfolding.

He had stayed back. An old lady was talking to him. Elegant, French perhaps. Her eyelids, a delicate bluish tone, were wide open, her gaze fixed on him. Her chin raised, every part of her thin little body tense, it was like fate, the future, something missing. Eventually she rewarded Solange with four words: 'You like Cindy Sherman?' The subtext, factual and depressing, was 'How lucky you are'.

Old women adored Kouhouesso. So did middle-aged women. And young women. Even little girls. Over the months to come, all those months swept along by the Big Idea, she would see countless little girls leap onto his knees, and countless old ladies, with the same naivety, force their way through crowds, come straight up to him, to ask if he liked contemporary art/the panpipe/rattan furniture/silkscreen painting.

*

Afterwards they went driving around Los Angeles. Driving

for the sake of driving, for the city, for the night. She liked his car, a Mercedes Coupé from the eighties. It smelled of him. Incense and tobacco. It was like huddling inside his embrace. Assimilated. Integrated. With a solid chassis, her seatbelt tight, and the luxury of letting her hair blow in the wind. And if they missed a turn, they would die together.

The voice of the GPS spoke for them. Beverly Glen Boulevard. Mulholland Drive. Ventura Freeway. Pronouncing names, names of places for which they had crossed the world. The ghosts for which they had emigrated. The city, way down there, glittering like a sky. And the letters of HOLLYWOOD in one direction, DOOWYLLOH in the other. The further they drove, the further they went back in time. The Observatory from *Rebel Without a Cause*. Silhouettes in the mist, palm trees from the fifties against a sky from the fifties. In the glow from the lighthouses, the mist rolled back over and over, the night welcomed them with every spin of their wheels. They were sinking into the Californian dream, and it was inexhaustible.

She remembered the interview with Cassavetes, in black and white, right here on Mulholland. Cassavetes so cool and sexy in his convertible under the bright light, Cassavetes who wanted to film *Crime and Punishment* as a musical comedy, Cassavetes saying of this town, 'People never meet here', and 'California Girls' starts up on the radio, starts right at the moment when the camera is filming Cassavetes. Start there, in life itself, in the present, forever, the Beach Boys forever as a soundtrack to Cassavetes direct from Hollywood time.

She looked at him side-on, at the wheel, in the hills at night. Yes, you could see it…the resemblance…the same mouth, the same forehead. Cassavetes as a black guy: without the dreadlocks, okay…but that irresistible feeling of déjà vu, that devastating *motion blur* where she kept on seeing faces she knew…The Cassavetes night had just fallen; Cassavetes was going home while they continued to drive, from that day to that night where she was here, in the canyons, with this man who looked so much like someone.

'*Crime and Punishment* as a musical comedy?' Kouhouesso shook his head. 'What a stupid idea.' According to him, it would have been a disaster: microphones in the fields, drunken actors, a hysterical Gena Rowlands, the place on Mulholland made up as a Russian log house. Once he had finished *Heart of Darkness*, he planned to shoot a musical—a serious project, about Miriam Makeba.

She assumed her knowing look. Fatigue hovered around them again; they would have to drive faster, leave behind this strange burden. He kept exceeding the speed limit (he hated automatic cars), he conceded that Cassavetes was probably brilliant, okay; but what about Polanski; what about Kubrick. Even Sydney Pollack. Professionals. Truly great filmmakers. The framework of cinema was a combination of genius and technical mastery. The New Wave had done a lot of damage to cinema.

She sniggered. 'Sydney Pollack!' He protested: he'd

mentioned Polanski first. Cassavetes' films were all over the shop, scraps of films, *trial* films. She praised the passion of his hysterical women, extolled the virtues of the unsuccessful films, films all the more brilliant for the flaws that illuminated them. He lit another cigarette, blew hard: he *despised* shoddy workmanship—the more he scorned the idea the more he rolled his *rs*—he would be the first filmmaker born in Africa to have the necessary resources, serious resources, professional resources!

She had never disagreed! The mist had dispersed. The night was sparkling, sharp and dry. He accelerated. Faster and faster, the GPS rattled off the list of places that were hastening her home. Wilshire, South Beverly Glen, Copa de Oro, Bellagio, end of the road. He parked in front of the metal gates of the apartment block, got out to open the door, but didn't turn off the engine. He was tired.

She begged him. She didn't want to go into her empty home by herself. No, he wasn't in the mood. He gestured with his arm for her to let go of him.

IL FAUT BEAUCOUP AIMER LES HOMMES

She watched *Dazzled* again. She forced herself to open books. She came across a sentence that she texted to him: 'We have to love men a lot. A lot, a lot. Love them a lot in order to love them. Otherwise it's impossible; we couldn't bear them. Marguerite Duras'

He didn't reply. Not five minutes later. Not three days later. She complained to Rose that he lacked a sense of humour.

'He'll contact you,' said Rose. She wanted to see a photo. Solange sent her an internet link: the clip of *Dazzled* that made her weak at the knees. Rose went into raptures over his good looks, compared him to George. One more handsome guy in Solange's already thriving love-life. She didn't push it too far.

Except that it wasn't one more guy in her life; it was life itself.

She searched through her computer history. Her computer that he often borrowed at night. And indeed he had nothing to hide: he was studying actors' record sheets and budgets, watching films, comparing cinematographers, investigating the feasibility of sound engineering in the forest, reading all he could about Conrad and the Congo, finding out about equatorial diseases, waterproof cameras, portable mosquito nets, drinking-water tanks, lightweight tents, plane tickets, film studios in Lagos and Capetown, the cost of an interpreter in places inhabited by the Baka people. 'Gwyneth Paltrow naked' was the one slightly jarring item in this coherent record. And also—lots of time spent correcting Wikipedia entries and discussing with other contributors, on the topic of Conrad or Makeba or even the catfish (with poisonous antennae) in the Ogooué River. He was the sole author of the entry 'King of Ife', in three languages. The length of the article demoralised her.

So that's what he was doing at night, instead of coming to bed with her?

His screenplay was also there, in a folder called *HOD*. *Heart of Darkness*. She typed in 'the Intended', and found nothing; she typed in 'Gwyneth' and the role appeared. Short: three pages, three scenes, three minutes. Scarcely more than what she'd done with Damon. Gwyneth wouldn't want it. Of course, there was George. And now Jessie. But even if Gwyneth had a gap in her schedule…three minutes for a first-time director?

She held her hair up in the mirror: an old-fashioned bun, a few loose strands. Very pale make-up. A dress with a corset, the bodice buttoned to the neck but fitted. 'No one knew him so well as I! I had all his noble confidence. I knew him best.' Softer, a whisper: 'No one knows him so well as I! I have all his noble confidence. I know him best…'

It was striking how so little of the novel was devoted to women or to Africans (so what role was Jessie going to play?). She thought about possible improvements. Everything changed if the Intended accompanied Kurtz to the Congo. She then became a particular type of expatriate woman: dashing and rebellious, close to the black people, both timid and sensual, stricken with boredom and with wonder. They got married there, in a little evangelical chapel. And when her man left the colonial army, she followed him, of course, into the heart of darkness.

She was the heart of darkness: it was her, with her kindness, her big heart, shining a light on the infernal sorcery of colonialism.

It was a magnificent role, encompassing the whole film. The type of role where she would be on the poster with George, like Isabelle Huppert with Kristofferson in *Heaven's Gate*. She sketched a few drafts of scenes and filed them in *HOD-2*.

A week had passed. She couldn't decide whether to call him or not.

*

Time took hold of her again. She was time's catfish, a fish from stagnant waters, a large fish from a slow river. She was decomposing. Lloyd had told her about a little role in *ER* but she wasn't sure. She had left a polite message on Steven Soderbergh's phone but he hadn't called back. At a dinner she surprised herself by not listening to a thing, until the word *Kinshasa* hit her like an explosion—the guests were amazed by her Congological knowledge. Had they heard about the new adaptation of *Heart of Darkness*? The conversation drifted on to Coppola, his daughter, his vineyards, and she stopped listening.

Dazzled by Michael Mann. She remembered that Lloyd had mentioned it to her at the time, but she'd been on the set of *Musette*, so it wouldn't have fitted in. A scene where the two cops burst into a French restaurant—she could have been the sexy waitress. Their paths would have crossed. Would she already have fallen for him? Or? *Synchronicity*: one of Kouhouesso's words. A practical man, who thinks in terms of compatible schedules. But she knew that—at any time, in Clèves, in Paris, in Los Angeles—at any time, she would have followed him.

No. She had found him handsome, that black guy who played Hamlet, not Othello, at Bouffes du Nord Theatre, but she had not gone out of her way to get to know him. She was twenty-two. She had crossed paths with the prince; it was unintentional. Or perhaps he was too princely for the Solange of that period.

The waitress in *Dazzled* ends up sleeping with the white guy. She couldn't remember a film, American or otherwise, in which a black guy and a white woman—a white guy and a black woman—sleep together without it being the subject itself of the drama. When a white guy and a black woman—a black guy and a white woman—get a bit too close, it's as if an alarm goes off, the public stiffens, the producers have said stop, the scriptwriters have already sorted out the issue, the black actor knows that he will not seduce the white actress: or else we're in another film, a morality tale, an affair, a problem.

She rewound…there…he's going to do it, he's going to turn towards the sea and the light stays with him, obscuring his expression, and he becomes the focus, becomes everything…That motion blur, that tiny degree of motion blur, like a photo stared at for too long…

Their world was *tolerant*. Hollywood, Paris, Manhattan: homosexual couples, threesome couples, couples where the man was older than the woman. A few white-Asian couples. But Asians are white. And who did Rihanna and Beyoncé go out with? With black guys. And then there was Halle Berry, who went out with a white guy, but her skin was much paler than Kouhouesso's. And she had seen photos of Lenny Kravitz with a Brazilian top model who, as white as she looked, was much darker than Solange.

Her head was starting to spin—like when you go through those wallpaper colour charts that look like giant phone directories of colours—from wondering if black is black. And she didn't have a clue.

TOM-TOM AT SOHO HOUSE

He called. His name came up on her phone. Yes, come. Yes, ring the buzzer. The lock turned by itself, magic: he opened it with the key she had given him. She wrapped her arms around him, right there, straightaway. He asked for a glass of water first; he'd played tennis and had a headache. A fever? A spot of sunstroke? She didn't know he played tennis. Or that he could get sunstroke. She put a wet cloth on his forehead. She kissed his eyelids gently. She fluttered her eyelashes against his cheeks, butterfly kisses, like her father used to give her when she was little. He fell asleep against her and she didn't dare move.

He was worried. Gwyneth's agent hadn't called. A week passed before they were told that she had other commitments. Jessie suggested Scarlett Johansson. Too voluptuous.

Ted could see Charlize in the role, with her aloofness. Too masculine, according to Kouhouesso.

They were at Soho House, at the edge of the square pond under the olive trees. Fifteen storeys below, the cars had discreetly hastened to make room for George and Jessie and their amazing vehicles. It was the first time she had been part of an *HOD* meeting. She didn't know if she was with Kouhouesso as his girlfriend or as an actress. Or because of the group's inertia? Or because, for George, she was obviously with them? Or because she was attractive? In the alcoholic languor of a late afternoon in Los Angeles, in the polluted heat, in the Californian pre-Christmas, she felt as beautiful and strong as a palm tree. The word *Intended* was whistling softly in her head.

The waitress came to take their orders. George gave the waitress the eye. The waitress laughed. She looked like Anne Hathaway. George's agent suggested Anne Hathaway. Jessie's agent boasted about one of his clients, Kelye, a little bit has-been. Eva Green would be better, said George's agent. Three starlets in fake Versace sat down at the next table. At the end of the terrace, near the fountain, Kate Bosworth was drinking a smoothie. She called out hi to George. A role was hovering over Hollywood, a role with its little wings, its flimsy little dress, its little 'where to land?' look. Los Angeles was starting to buzz, to raise a fine golden dust on its crackleware back.

The waitress moved off. The fish in the pond darted around and the men talked. An English girl? Keira Knightley? A clever and classy European girl? A French girl? Ted said the name Audrey Tautou four times. Jessie suggested Catherine Deneuve, young. Jessie's agent said Julie Delpy. Ted said Audrey Tautou for the fifth time.

Kouhouesso looked at her. She gave him her audition smile. He looked at her as he did often: his head slightly tilted, mildly worried, as if he was surprised she was there. Or else (the idea suddenly struck her) he, too, was trying to work it out. Since the beginning. Who she looked like. That face. Those eyes.

He had tied back his dreadlocks. He was wearing a thin cashmere sweater, pale turquoise, nothing underneath, and a scarf of yellow linen. He seemed even taller and almost skinny, apart from the breadth of his shoulders under the mass of hair. Jessie suggested Kim Wilde. When she was young. He'd be happy to have young Kim Wilde for himself. Ted was sulking. Kouhouesso called the waitress for a second Eastern Standard (vodka-tonic cucumber-mint) and excused himself to go out for a cigarette. George took Solange by the elbow and led her out to the terrace, on the heels of Kouhouesso.

A thick layer of red mist was lying over Los Angeles like blush. Kouhouesso was leaning against the guardrail, the smoke from his cigarette merging with the fog. Sunset Boulevard was spread out fifteen storeys below, as if, simply by extending his arms, Kouhouesso himself had thrown a spotlight on it.

George said that she, Solange, would be perfect as the Intended. 'She would no doubt be perfect,' joked Kouhouesso, 'but first I have to see her naked.' Everyone gave a bit of a laugh. George raised his finger, a waitress appeared. He ordered champagne, but Kouhouesso, who steered clear of mixing his drinks, stuck with his Eastern Standard. The terrace was a raft floating on the fog.

Then Kouhouesso started to tell a slightly strange story, in which he recounted that he hadn't wanted to be tactless to a certain girl at a certain party, not knowing if she was with someone and possibly him, George, in any case not knowing if he wasn't over-interpreting the signals he received, aware that he was experiencing a certain level of tension, by no means unpleasant (he smiled at the red fog) but anxious, first and foremost, not to come across as inappropriate, because, in this world where nothing is left unsaid, he made it a point of honour to leave each person to his, or her, private life: what did he know in fact about that girl? Nothing, and he would have rather been struck down by lightning that night than risk the slightest impropriety.

It was as if he had wanted to communicate something to them, a secret, a declaration, but the message was lost. As for the Intended, the casting slipped back into limbo.

There was a bit of a commotion inside. Jessie had spilled his drink down his Gucci suit and the waitresses were buzzing around him. Ted had gone, no one knew where. They were discussing Jessie's role, which was now clearer: Kouhouesso had developed the character of the steamboat driver, only two pages in the novel, but probably the most racist pages. Jessie wouldn't stop reading the description out loud, at the top of his voice, in Soho House: 'an improved specimen', 'a dog in a parody of breeches and a feather hat, walking on his hind legs'! Kouhouesso and he were having a good laugh. She and George gazed at the fish. 'A fucking racist masterpiece!' yelled Jessie. Kouhouesso, magnanimous and instructional, spoke about period and narrative: Marlow's point of view on negroes, whereas these days George or Solange...'A fucking racist masterpiece!' Jessie repeated. The word *negro* reverberated like a bell in Solange's already painful skull.

They had to find a name for this cannibal: Kouhouesso put forward 'Iyapo', the name of his grandfather, Iyapo meaning 'many troubles'. Everyone laughed. The pitfalls would be more numerous than the mosquitoes in the rainy season.

So there was a grandfather. She wondered if everyone in the family had names ending in *o*. Did 'Kouhouesso' mean something? Her French teacher had taught her, around the time when the whole high school was wearing 'SOS Racism' badges, that it was impolite to ask the meaning of names. George means George. Solange doesn't mean either Sol ('soil') or Ange ('angel'), but comes from the Latin, *solennis*.

Only white people would assume that savages have names that mean 'little cloud in the wind' or that sort of thing. Back then, she didn't dare point out to her teacher that her second name, Oïhana, meant 'forest' in Basque. The Basque people are the Africans of Europe.

The character of Iyapo-Jessie had to be stoking the boiler on the boat during the whole trip up the river. Which meant three weeks in the Congo for Jessie. He had taken off his stained jacket and undone the top buttons of his shirt. His agent suggested that he go back two or three times, but would that fit in with *Angry Men 4*? And what about the promotional tour for *Return of Scissors*? 'Fuck the promotion,' Jessie said loudly, and he lit up a joint right there on the terrace. Kouhouesso explained that you can't just 'go back two or three times' to central Congo. The caves he had in mind for Kurtz's station were only accessible by helicopter. 'Does Ted know that?' asked George. His own window of time was only a week; the dates for *Sailor's 13* were scheduled, as was the second film he was directing. Kouhouesso looked up to the sky: 'Santa Rita, pray for me.' A waitress brought Jessie an ashtray and apologised on behalf of the management: the person delivering the new suit was stuck in traffic. Jessie took off his shirt.

His girlfriend had turned up. Her name was Alma— enormous breasts and about eighteen years old. Jessie read her the description of Iyapo, filed teeth and a piece of polished bone stuck through his lower lip. Alma ordered a room-temperature latte, not too hot, not too cold, easy enough, no? In the end, the role of Kurtz-George was the least problematic: it was crucial, but all concentrated at the end of the film. Except that his scene was supposed to be shot on site, at the caves, and the insurance was delaying things: George was worth a mint. The casting for Marlow was underway: they were waiting for an answer from Sean Penn. Jessie was tom-tomming on a bar stool; in a minute he was going to jump on a table and shout, naked and beating his chest. George was laughing. There were more cocktails on the house.

Solange said she could make herself available at any time, including the Congo shoot, but no one seemed to hear her. Her cheeks were burning and her belly was tied in knots. Jessie-Iyapo launched into a southern nursery rhyme, *Old MacDonald had a farm, ee i ee i oh*...His suit had arrived; Alma was helping him put it on among a swarm of waitresses. The sun was plunging down over the city, red and flat like an ecstasy tablet.

THE FREEDOM OF THE SAVANNAH

It was a stifling December. Jessie was by the pool the whole time. By *his* pool. Alma was there, too. Otherwise, no one really knew where she lived. Inside her phone, apparently. Jessie told her off. It was a long-term educational undertaking: 'It's really bad manners to be on your phone when you're with someone. If you were a man, you'd be a jerk. Which person are you prioritising? Think about it: the one who is absent, or the one who is physically present? Can you really count the time you spend on the phone as *quality time*? Do you consider that you are *with* the person to whom you are speaking at a distance? Do you really consider that you can call it *time spent together* when it's on the phone?'

In Solange's opinion, he overused the interrogative. And when he kept going, making quotation mark signs with his fingers, she screwed up her eyes in pain. 'Don't you think the *physical* presence is the most important part? You don't speak to someone in the same way when their body is *absent* as you do when their body is *present*. Haven't you ever felt the difference? I mean, physically? Politeness is not *just* words, politeness is what you owe to the *physical* presence of the other: you respect your own body, so when you're on the phone it's the same thing. Your priority should be the person who is *present*, in the full meaning of the word…'

He was a real proselytiser, and taught her, among other things, the meaning of the word *proselytiser*. The problem was that there was no pool without Jessie. For the moment, one went with the other. He was between shoots.

The Mexican gardeners were busy spreading fresh bark mulch around the flowerbeds. Hummingbirds flitted from flower to flower, magically suspended in the air here and there. The rose bushes had all reflowered, in the middle of December, like an early or very late spring—no one knew anymore. They spoke about the weather; they spoke about the fact that they no longer spoke in the same way about the climate. They spoke about the end of the world, not scheduled by the Mayans but by our own irresponsible behaviour. The maid brought them grapefruit-vodka cocktails. Alma sent hers back, some temperature issue. Kouhouesso was still asleep. Or else he'd had his coffee but he had to be left alone. No sound came from upstairs. She wondered if he was correcting Wikipedia entries.

They had learnt the day before that the key producer, who had signed on because of George's name alone, had pulled out after reading the script. Coppola had done immense damage to Conrad: a legendary film, certainly, but above all a budgetary apocalypse. And no one wanted to insure George in the Congo. No one could imagine Jessie in the Congo. And no one wanted to do sound engineering in the Congo. In fact, no one wanted to hear the word Congo. That's what Hollywood was there for, to reinvent the Congo—in the studio. As well as the boat. The BBC was said to be interested, but the idea of a *real* boat made them back off; they could already see Kouhouesso as Werner Herzog, drowning in a river of pounds sterling. And there was no news from Sean Penn. And Anne Hathaway was overbooked.

Everything was foundering, like a steamboat without wood for fuel, a vessel that was all set up, designed, constructed, the river ahead and the enormous forest around, but whose crew, only just put together, had disappeared into thin air. Kouhouesso's phone didn't ring anymore. George was the only one encouraging him to refine his script while he had free time. It's the freedom of the savannah, said Kouhouesso. I'm not free of anything.

The only area in which he could still do something was in the casting. Marlow was on hold, nothing was being said about the Intended, but for the black actress he had a series of meetings with African-American women, Nigerian women from Hollywood, Caribbean women, and even the

97

Surinamese woman from George's party.

'What Surinamese woman?'

'The Surinamese woman from George's party.'

'Lola? The one who was in *Lost*? She's not black.'

'Of course she's black.'

Lola Behn. On her Wikipedia entry she was 71% European, 26% African, and 3% Orinico Delta Warao Indian from Venezuela. She had been part of the Roots DNA testing program. Twenty-six per cent, according to Kouhouesso, made her clearly a black person: 'For white people, if you're not completely white, you are black; for mixed-race people, that's never the case.'

She felt as if she was hearing the famous old stand-up joke on TV about washing powders that wash 'whiter than white' and 'less white than white'. Didn't he know it?

No. He never spoke about his childhood. It was clear from his lack of connection with the others, from the signs of non-recognition, that he had not danced to Kim Wilde in his adolescence, not drunk Malibu pineapple cocktails, never had a skateboard or a Walkman, never watched MTV, and had no idea about the pop singers and TV hosts who were the idols of her youth.

*

As soon as he left, he disappeared again. Two days, six days, ten days. She waited for him. And he came back. He always came back.

She didn't like the idea that he had meetings with all those black girls, each one more beautiful and younger than the one before.

She had asked him for one word of certainty. But he wasn't at a point in his life when he could commit. Because of the film. 'Solange, the only commitments I know are the ones from people in this profession.' One of the stories that made him laugh was the way Steve McQueen, Al Pacino, Robert Redford and Jack Nicholson all pussyfooted around Coppola: by saying neither yes nor no when he was casting *Apocalypse Now*, they had driven him crazy.

Solange. He had said her name: 'Solange, the only commitments I know are the ones from people in this profession.' Proper pronunciation, with the nasal *–ange.* It was the first time. When he wasn't using 'hey' he called her 'Sugar' or 'Babe', cute, cheeky names, always in English. But: Solange. It was proof, if not of love, at least of affection. And he had kissed her, *smack.*

Every night he went back to his script, not in order to de-Congolise it, but so that on the first day of shooting all his energy would be available for any unexpected events caused by the forest. And by Jessie, she wanted to add.

The freedom of the savannah (she learned on the Internet) was what a slave was granted informally, without emancipation papers.

CRASH TEST

'He's going round in circles,' Jessie said to her, brooding. 'Ever since you spoke to him about Godard, all he does is play tennis.' Jessie, one on one, turned out to be so much shrewder than when he was with Alma. For some reason she couldn't fathom, most men only revealed themselves properly when they were talking to her alone. Rose had always attested to this: there was something about her that allowed even the most difficult individuals to open up.

Wearing white shorts, Kouhouesso crossed the path, heading to his car. The Mexican doorman opened the metal security gate for him. She stayed there. She didn't dare go away: she never knew when she'd see him again. And she wasn't absolutely certain that, with Alma around, Jessie would receive her.

She arranged a dinner for him with Peter Maximovitch, a longstanding friend she had met through Chabrol. David Steinberg from *The Sopranos* was there, and Gaspar Melchior from HBO, and the guys from ClickStar, who might be interested. Kouhouesso announced that he would only accept money from television on the condition that he had total creative freedom, a 'final cut' clause set in stone, and Maximovitch, who was well acquainted with madness, looked at him with admiration, expert as he was in self-sabotage and deliberate scuttling. When Bob Evans arrived, very late and very old, on the arm of a very young nurse in a very short uniform, Solange looked at Kouhouesso expectantly: the Golden Age of Hollywood was there. He stayed silent. Peter told a story she already knew, about a joyride on the occasion of the launch of his first film: Coppola post–*Godfather*, in his enormous limousine, Friedkin post–*The Exorcist*, who was sticking his head out of the roof, and Peter, in his beaten-up Volvo, racing them on Sunset Boulevard and all of them yelling *me me me*—a classic competition to see who could piss the furthest.

But weariness seemed to have caught up with Kouhouesso. The evening subsided into chatter about the weather: Bob was worried that the nurse was feeling the heat. Peter had never known such a sweltering December since he'd arrived in Los Angeles, the very first winter of the seventies.

The winter I was born, thought Solange. In Clèves, a long way from here.

Was it such a bad idea to have wanted to introduce him to the dinosaurs, to the witnesses of a time when Hollywood was one huge party? A cinephile like him should have been fascinated. Sure, his project was stalling, but they had all been through bad times, too. In the nineties, Maximovitch used to walk down Hollywood Boulevard with his starched mauve shirt and his bandana knotted in a floppy bowtie. *Do you remember me? I was Peter Maximovitch.* He would get himself photographed on exactly the spot where the statue of Shrek stands today. But he had lived on so long after his downfall that he had become a kind of idol. Personally, she worshipped him. He would have made a magnificent Kurtz, thin, lined, arrogant: more Kinski than Brando. If he'd survived Hollywood, the Congo wouldn't be the end of him.

She was joking around; she'd had too much to drink. Less than Kouhouesso, but too much. At this point in the conversation, he was sunk in his habitual silence, but the rest of the gang were all laughing; Peter, defying his age, was pretending to be Tarzan on an imaginary vine.

Then Kouhouesso spoke, only a few words, unequivocally, with incongruous force, in a tone that was almost brutal: 'George will play Kurtz.'

'Has George signed anything?' Gaspar asked out of interest.

Kouhouesso stood up. She felt obliged to follow him out, excusing herself. Everything was spinning. As she hurried past, she said *sorry, sorry* to the walls, to the wait staff.

When she replayed the evening in her mind, she felt ashamed; she wasn't sure exactly of what, and that was even more unpleasant.

She remembered the times when her father was intractable, simultaneously flamboyant and mute. Her mother's ghastly smile. Now she found herself having to 'form a buffer', as her mother used to say. Between Kouhouesso and the world. But every single project in Hollywood had to undergo a dreadful blowtorch of criticism. Every director is interrogated, people have to see what they're made of: it's the mandatory crash test for every aspiring filmmaker.

In the car on the way home, the silence was that of their unique weariness; like a third person in their duo, this weariness loaded up in the back of the car, weariness like a child, which could at any moment leap at them and cause them to tumble into a ravine of anguish and hatred—yes, of hatred, a silent and suppressed hatred, a weary hatred. 'Talk to me,' she begged. She was drunk at the wheel, but they were in Bel Air, not far from her place, which, in her state, was spinning less than Topanga. He was falling asleep. Their weariness was ebbing back towards the east, into the first rays of the dawn.

When they arrived in front of the gate, he wanted to go home to his place. He shook his head. This was serious non-cooperation. She went round to the other side of the car and made him get out. She struggled against the weight of him, against gravity; she struggled against whatever force was holding him there, upright, unmoving, heavy, supported by the Earth and by hell, protesting in a language she didn't understand; he was so much bigger than her, so much stronger than her. She heard sirens—how ridiculous, a breathalyser test right in front of her place? Blue and white lights flashing, spinning. Kouhouesso was pressed against the bonnet, the cops repeating the same question: 'Is this man bothering you?' She had no idea what was going on. Kouhouesso was yelling. She was terrified.

The concierge came to their rescue. He opened the gate, explained to the cops that the two of them were together and went back to his cupboard for the keys.

At two in the afternoon of their morning after, Kouhouesso woke up with a 'hey'. On the television, thirty-nine high-school students had been killed with heavy weapons. By a boy: it was never by a girl. She wanted to get on a plane, put some space between her and America. She stroked his shoulder, but Kouhouesso shook himself, unhooked her hand as if it were an insect.

In an apocalyptic sunset, she took the car and fled to Olga's. They talked all night long, girl talk. The next day she drove aimlessly around Los Angeles. Her tears flowed over the intensely blue sky, into the dust of that month of December. Her tears flowed over the hills, over their savannah dryness and the strip of green, the lush edge of the gardens. She drove to the sea. In tears, she handed her keys to a Venice Beach parking valet. She sat on the low wall in front of the stupid, sloshing, dirty-grey ocean. Surfers were settled on the surface like seagulls. Choking sobs rose and fell in her throat. There was a *pop pop* sound coming from behind her: the pelota players were hard at it, whacking their ball against the graffitied walls. It was like being in Biarritz in the off-season, when she was fifteen with no future. Except that life had moved on, and come to a stop here, on the edge of the Pacific.

She drove towards Topanga. The door opened: he was there. He had looked for her—where had she gone? Ted had called on behalf of George. A budget had been released to finance the storyboard. She guessed that George had footed the bill.

He took her out for dinner. They had lobster, baked oysters, Chablis, Saint-Julien. He was smiling again. He told her that she and he were tarred with the same brush: they thought only of themselves. Of their own personal advantage. It was all about being a black man and a white woman, not just a man and a woman: she had to get used to it; neither he nor she was to blame. The problem dated back to the round-ups in the forests. He thought her friends were unbearable. Hollywood legends, my arse. They were members of a club and they would never let him join. His experience proved to him that, because of their history, their cultural fluency, their sharp minds, Jews were definitely not the most racist among white people…She objected. He stopped her, she was too French, locked into her own prejudices, let him finish. As usual during those dinners, he found it difficult to single out one particular sentence that was truly racist—well, he had a hunch, but let's not go there—it was everything, and it was done on purpose: you can never pass sentence on your enemy, he's caught up inside his whole worldview, his top-dog/underdog ideology of dominance. It was the obstacle that wore him down, the wall they erected without even realising, their world that they took to be the universe. *Universal Pictures presents!* He knew it by heart. And if they'd added a white guy, whether he was Jewish or not, who cares, and if they'd added another fucking Hollywood legend or a fucking young producer, the wall would have grown higher, expanded, exponentially. He needed Jessie. He needed Favour. Favour Adebukola Moon: the black actress who stood out from the crowd. He needed George and he needed her, too; but—he laughed—he was wary. He was wary of everyone. Even Favour. He laughed again. She paid the bill.

BLACK LIKE ME

Jessie lent them his bungalow at Malibu: an eight-room villa on the beach. The storyboard guy came every day; they locked themselves away to sketch out, frame by frame, the film Kouhouesso envisioned. Once the guy left, late at night, Kouhouesso would open bottles of wine and sit in front of the laptop he'd just bought himself. She would go to bed alone. She ended up missing Jessie's garrulous proselytism. Lloyd didn't understand why she'd turned down *ER*. She didn't dare tell him that she was waiting for the dates of an unlikely role in a dangerous film in an impossible country. In the Congo.

The rest of the time, Kouhouesso sat under the sunshade, facing the ocean, iPod in his ears or mobile phone on his knees. The film remained in the realm of the virtual;

the storyboard drawings were more to reassure potential producers than to plan actual shots. She went walking along the beach at low tide; she would look at him, a seated figure behind the guardrail, stuck in a dream house, in his very own Congo, with a woman who was waiting only for him.

What's he like, a man waiting? His head bent, heavy with alcohol and impatience. Consumed by the film shoot in his mind, by the images on paper. Rubbing his eyes with the flat of his hand, drawing on his immense weariness. She would hold out her hand, but he wouldn't take it. It was never the right time. Or rather it was always just when she was finally thinking about something else, or getting ready to swim, walk, read, that he would come up to her and put his arms around her. And afterwards he never said much. She complained about his moods. He accused her of calling what wasn't her business a *mood*: 'If I stop believing in it, who will believe in it for me?'

'George,' she replied.

She went down to the beach every day, for the pleasure of the beach, right there below the house. If it weren't for this film, this obsession, they would have been happy. She had begun cooking. She would have liked to have a dog to walk. She had got to know some of the locals in the area. You couldn't really call the strip of luxury villas between the sea and the highway a neighbourhood. A lot of them had dogs (even though it was illegal), a lot of them smoked (ditto), and they were easy to talk to. There was a Ukrainian guy and a Chinese woman who had met in a psychiatric hospital and loved to talk about it; a bodysurfing grandmother who was always trying to get her granddaughters minded; a depressive architect who couldn't stand his clients anymore; a mysterious Greek woman who sermonised in the dunes. The impoverished, who lived almost on the beach, and the super-wealthy, who also lived there, but differently.

A French couple recognised her, despite her hat and sunglasses. They had landed there for their retirement, on stilts, like herons. They were keen to invite her over for dinner; she smiled politely. She imagined Kouhouesso in their exquisite decor—in the end, only she could put up with him.

On the weekend the beach turned democratic: more people, more families, including the servants of the surrounding houses. As well as those venturing from the east side of the city, who had driven since morning in order to spend Sunday at Malibu. Black families armed with enormous rubber rings, Fritos, beach umbrellas, and grandmothers sitting on folding chairs. The boys (like Jessie but very different from Jessie) went swimming without taking off their gold chains, and most of the time without knowing how to swim, which made the lifeguards in their sentry box nervous. Without much of an idea how to, she wanted to make friends with these people. She complimented the grandmothers on their grandchildren. She shared chips with them and chatted about the weather, often unable to grasp their accent, whereas she understood Jessie and Kouhouesso, and Favour the Nigerian girl, and Lola from Suriname.

Being separated from Kouhouesso, even for a few hours, gave her the illusion, while she was with the black families, of somehow being with him. Yes, the familiarity was surprising. But perhaps it was not so much connected with Kouhouesso as with a déjà vu of her memories of the Basque Country, of her own adolescence. The fat grandmothers and the folding chairs. The ugly swimsuits, the towels that were not proper large beach towels but old rags from the bathroom cupboard. She remembered those occasional beach days, an hour's drive away, with her, say, boyfriend at the time, whom she was ashamed of, and the other girls on the beach, the—she thought about it, the white girls—the girls from Paris, the wealthy tourist girls; when she thought she was too fat and badly dressed, whereas—she knew now—she was the prettiest, the real princess. And she liked these girls at Malibu—a day out at Malibu—speaking too loudly to feel uncomfortable, with their ten-dollar Target swimsuits that were bad copies of expensive labels, and the enormous ice boxes, and the strollers in the sand. And the babies.

She had never held a black baby in her arms ('a little prune', her mother used to say if she saw one on the TV). She had never chatted about sunscreens with black girls, or even imagined that they, too, used protection against UV radiation. But she, too, had owned one good T-shirt that she kept for special occasions. Far from here, two oceans away.

Some older adolescents came to ask her if she was an

actress. They flirted with her. It would never have happened in her previous life. Unimaginable. Until now, she had never spoken, either in Paris or Los Angeles, with one of those tall guys in hoodies. But she was no longer frightened. Anyway, she was old enough to be their mother.

In 1960, scarcely ten years before the heyday of Friedkin and Coppola, the journalist John H. Griffin, disguised as a black man for his memoir, *Black Like Me*, had been warned by his black friends: never look at a white woman, *even* a woman on a film poster. Asking for trouble. In California, the last lynching had taken place in 1947. The fellow had been caught on a ranch near Gazelle, and hanged in front of the only school in the area, in Callahan.

STORYBOARD IN MALIBU

And yet the film began to take shape, but as a cartoon strip.
A crowded sketch: the forest, the shadows and the water, in
black and white. The boat's lantern made a cone of light on
the black water and the rest of the vessel was like a whale
surfacing, grey on black, among the islands and sandbanks.
Tracks hacked out by machete, the glow of oil lamps, torches
that left the black people in shadow and highlighted the
ivory and gold, and the dazzling fires, and the night in the
sacred caves. Marlow's face on almost every page, a white
patch, a halo, like a ghost: Kouhouesso did not want him
to have any features. He was still hoping for Sean Penn.
The first appearance of George as Kurtz was a close-up of
his sweaty face, then a tracking shot of his long thin body.
George said he was up for losing ten kilos; Kouhouesso

joked about the efficacy of local dysentery.

The director of photography and the chief lighting engineer came to work in Malibu for the day. Over the sound of the waves, she heard incoherent bursts of shouting, Kouhouesso's deep voice, brusque. When they came out of the study they barely acknowledged her and did not stay for dinner. There were pages of the storyboard, around the time Kurtz dies, where all the panels were black, with just a few white embers, and eyes, and teeth. Kouhouesso wanted to work with natural light, which meant the images would be not only dark but blurred, as only lightweight cameras were possible in the forest.

The sea rose, indifferent. High tides, waves breaking right onto the terrace; the noise was deafening under the stilts. He stayed inside, the shutters closed, in the dark, the sun outside exploding for no one at all.

Her country of choice was not the Congo but this beach, now so familiar, so Basque, with Los Angeles as a hazy background. She knew that at any moment she could join him: he was there, waiting, immobilised, in the house on stilts.

She chatted with the surfers. Most of them drove for hours to come searching for waves, sets not found anywhere else in the world. Then they stood on the dunes to get dry, among the empty cans and other bodies. Upright, like cormorants, gazing out at the waves they'd just left. She had already seen that look on some of the surfers in Biarritz:

on adults, the ones whose lives were consumed by surfing. And she said to herself: perhaps that's what it is. Perhaps that's what I recognise. That burnt-out look, fixed eyes, blazing, obsessed by the horizon, in this impossible man, Kouhouesso, my love.

*

Only once did she manage to drag him onto the sand, at sunset, after the storyboard guy had left and after a few glasses of wine. She was tanned, happy. Life would run its course right here, far from the Congo. She was wearing her white dress, the one with the straps and the crocheted bodice, and her big straw hat and sun-bleached braids. He was smiling, like magic, out of the blue. Yes, she was funny, and lively, and irresistible, and he was in love—he had to be, or else? Or else, why was he here?

He stopped at the edge of the water, dipped his toes in. 'Come on!' she said, and pulled off her dress—bikini, I am Raquel Welch—and dived straight into the waves with a powerful freestyle. He raised his phone and took a photo of her: smile.

They would soon be celebrating six months together (he was amazed when she told him). And she had never managed to get him into the water, not the jacuzzi, not the pool, and definitely not the sea. He told her that salt damaged dreadlocks. He washed them once a week, ceremoniously, then spent a long time drying them: he worried about mould. Afterwards, the bathroom smelled of incense. He had travelled in India and Nepal; he must have brought back some kind of herbal ointment, or from God knows what African shop.

*

The storyboard draughtsman delivered the four last panels: windows, daytime, a side table, the town. A pale face, a black corseted dress, a tight bun: it was her. Bathed in an unearthly glow. The precise curve of her body, her small breasts, her long nose, high cheekbones and forehead: her exactly. She had the role. That's how she found out.

Christmas was in three days. The only information she'd managed to glean from Kouhouesso was that on the day of her Air France flight he had a meeting with an assistant producer.

That morning she woke early. The smooth sea reflected the green sky, and the muzzles of two sea lions were bobbing in the wake of the waves. Without the sea lions it would have been difficult to know where exactly the sea was—or if the sky were not filling up the entire Pacific Ocean. She made herself a coffee on the terrace, sent a few text messages over there, to France. Then she rolled herself a joint and put on her sunglasses, staring eastwards, directly at the sun. Every minute, a plane took off from LAX, at the spot where the coast was flat, in the heart of the city. Up high they left long white streaks, lines of cocaine gradually crisscrossing the space in every direction. At 11.20 a.m., she watched a minuscule plane rising slowly, over there, without a sound; she knew that plane leaving without her was the 11.20 a.m. for Paris CDG, immediately followed by another plane, then another, none of which she was in, as though minute by minute she was being shot into the sky, virtually, while still clinging here like a mollusc on the stilts of the house.

Kouhouesso didn't move all day.

The good news was that Oprah Winfrey might be interested. Production was starting up again.

ANGOLA IS A PARTY

The evening they returned to Topanga Canyon, they found
the house completely lit up, thirty cars parked out the front,
a gigantic pine tree erected on the edge of the swimming
pool. Jessie, bare-chested, white beard and red boxer shorts,
was greeting guests and handing out little bowls full of
some sort of snow in which adorable dwarf pines were
planted. The dwarf pines were made out of chocolate and
the powder snow was intended for snorting. It took a few
moments to decipher Alma's outfit: a bra made out of grey
fur, Playboy Bunny hotpants, Nubuck leather Timberland
boots, and a leather muzzle with reins that Jessie cracked on
her naked back, for fun. Perhaps the most disturbing thing
was the strange headdress tied to her head: gold antlers, a
Spike TV trophy for the prize she had just received: 'Most

Promising Sexy TV Star—Men's Choice.'

'She's wearing a reindeer costume,' Jessie explained, as if it was obvious. He pretended to straddle her. 'Father Christmas is going down your chimney, my darling. He has a big present for you.'

They fled upstairs. Fortunately no one was hanging out in the loft, but the music from below was too loud. And it was freezing up there: so that he could have a roaring fire in the fireplace, Jessie had turned the air conditioning on full bore all over the house.

They headed back to her place. Kouhouesso was silent, as he was every time he was annoyed by reality. She tried to stay quiet too, but she couldn't. They had to face facts: when Jessie was there, it was tricky living together. The practical solution was for Kouhouesso to move in with her for good.

In the meantime, she placed two plane tickets for Paris under their Christmas tree. She had bought two more tickets, full-price business. They wouldn't get there until the 26th. But now that her son was older, Christmas Day itself didn't matter as much.

He gave her a peck on the lips. But he wasn't sure: he really had to find time, before the shoot, to go and see his children.

In Luanda.

In Angola.

She had assumed he was born in Cameroon.

Twins. Who lived with their mother. Their stepfather was from Rio.

She made a quick adjustment to the world-map app in her head, skipping from one latitude to the next, leaving a large, blurry area over Angola. She pictured child soldiers, wearing dirty, oversized T-shirts, children from shanty towns, glue-sniffers, and prostitutes.

Hollywood–Angola, Los Angeles–Luanda, LAX–LAD: there was a plane every day. Direct. British Airways.

But, now that he thought of it, the twins would be in Lisbon for New Year. Their mother was Portuguese. And Lisbon was right next to Paris.

Paris–Lisbon!

No distance at all, she enthused, championing Europe's modest size, extolling the speed of the TGV, the quality of the freeways, the Maastricht Treaty and budget airfares. Whereas Luanda was so far away.

And so expensive, added Kouhouesso. There was nowhere under four hundred dollars a night. Compared with Rio, which was half the price, and half the distance.

She wanted to say that he wouldn't be in a hotel in Paris, but everything was moving too fast to get hung up on the geography.

The mother divided her time between Rio, Luanda and Lisbon, the three ports in Lusitanian waters. As for the twins, they lived in the Miami, one of the nightclubs frequented by the Luanda jetset, on a peninsula, right on the water.

A girl and a boy on a Facebook page, out-of-this-world good-looking, illuminated in red, green, blue, silver, spangled by glitter balls, fireworks and fairy lights—they seemed to be in their habitat. Spin the globe as fast as you can: that's the colour of the future. Luanda is a party. Rio is finished. Lisbon is dead. The twins both fell in love for the first time in Luanda: that's the problem with adolescents, according to Kouhouesso: they get *settled*, much more than their parents do.

With all these images piling up inside her skull, she couldn't think of anything else to say, other than how beautiful his children were. *There's no such thing as mixed race*: she knew what happened with sentences like that, sentences he uttered. They led to another image, a baby who might have been theirs, Kouhouesso and Solange, Solange and Kouhouesso.

She really should tell him about her son. But she still had two more days.

'THE STAKE OF DEATH HAS BEEN PLANTED', 'WE HAVE THROWN AWAY THE HOE' AND 'THERE ARE NO MORE NAMES LEFT'

Kouhouesso had seen Oprah. And Oprah had seen Kouhouesso: she agreed to be a co-producer. The film shoot would be on a boat, following the chronology of the novel: leaving from the Thames in a schooner, navigating the coast of West Africa, then upriver in a little steamboat. If not in the Congo—let's be reasonable—then in Gabon or in southern Cameroon: better logistics, fewer heavy weapons. Kouhouesso pulled a face, but Canal Plus was coming on board. And the screenplay had been sent to Vincent Cassel.

'It's going to be shot in the Congo,' he said to her. Yes, to her. She focused less on the hubris of his assertion than on the fact that he trusted her and was confiding in her. They were smoking a joint in bed, their bags packed for Paris. The flight was the next day. *Kouhouesso in the Congo*. She smiled. A good antidote to Tintin. Kouhouesso had never set foot in the Congo, any more than she had. For him, too, it was the unknown. For him, too, it was *Africa*: jungle, untouched, inaccessible. For both of them: no asphalt, no guardrails. Being Kouhouesso—being black—did not immunise him against anything.

From what she had gleaned, he was born in a relatively arid area of Cameroon (she'd only recently learnt that there were *arid* areas in Cameroon). He was about two when he ran away from the concession. His mother found him, dead, stiff and dried out like a log of wood. She took him to the medicine woman, but the medicine woman said she needed to take him to the witch. He was probably under a spell. There was only one witch in the valley and she did nothing for less than a goat. The father was violently opposed to the expense and to resorting to such extremes; he was a rational man and didn't want to hear anything about spirits, from either the natives or anyone else. But Kouhouesso was still dead and looking more and more like a log of Assemela hardwood; he was getting harder and blacker before their eyes, turning into charcoal. When there was nothing but powder left of him, his mother sneaked away from the other wives, taking the family's only goat with her.

While his mother set off towards the hollow tree where

the witch lived, with him dead and the goat on a leash, a never-ending stream of car headlights disappeared behind the Hotel Bel-Air. She asked him if it was a traditional folk tale. Traditional of what? He laughed. Of the suffering of mothers, perhaps, she thought. She could picture her own mother lying down between her two aluminium bedside tables from the 1970s. But Kouhouesso's childhood seemed to be from an earlier time, as far in the past as she and he were in the future, bathed in the cone of light from the Bel Air cars. Cars that were not going to take him away, and into which he would not disappear—him, speaking now, alive and well, in her arms.

The witch took the goat and studied what was left of the dead child. She said that the child's name was Kouhouesso, that he had several other names but Kouhouesso was his real name. That he was an only child, but not the first. That his mother had had other children before him.

All that was true, the absolute truth. The witch said he was one of the children from a series of abikus. An abiku is a spirit child who lodges itself in the belly of women and is born in order to die, over and over again. As long as the spirit child is not recognised for what it is—an evil, tormenting and unrelenting creature—he will come back to blight hopes and promises.

The witch said that she would keep the child for as long as was necessary, but that it cost more for abikus: they would need to bring another goat. Otherwise, although the child would live, it would stay crouching under the roots, waiting to be reborn as an abiku.

So Kouhouesso spent days and nights in the hollow tree with the witch. When his mother returned, he was well and truly alive: he had got some colour back, and had even put on weight. Two fresh cuts, little triangles, were forming scars on his forehead. The witch told them to coat the scars with soot. Scarification was part of the treatment.

According to the adult Kouhouesso, bearer of triangles on his forehead, while he was in the tree, the old woman had buried him up to his neck in the moist, loose earth, the rich humus under the hollow tree, and she persevered in feeding him a mixture of water and milk, drop by drop, into his little mouth, just like the Fulani people do in the case of severe dehydration—and the Khoisan, the Tuareg, the Songhai, the Berabiche, the Reguibat, the Toubou, the Hausa, the Toucouleur, and the Australian Aborigines.

During all those days and all those nights, at church, and before altars, his mother had offered up prayers—prayers of struggle. And she had argued at length with his father, insisting that he sell an acre of wine palm trees in order to purchase another goat. The father had protested that it was a case of kidnapping and ransom, and that he would go himself to get his son, dead or alive. But some strange phenomenon prevented him: he kept banging into an invisible wall. He tried to leave the house but found himself laid out on the floor like a drunkard, his forehead swollen with unsightly bumps. So the mother took the opportunity to carry out the goat-acre transaction and to recover her son, Kouhouesso, who right now was speaking to Solange on a Los Angelean night.

He claimed to be able to remember the smell of goat on the witch, and a sensation of being enveloped in the damp, dark softness. Henceforth, he no longer needed *anything or anyone.*

Solange assured him that it was an intrauterine memory, a metaphor for a lost state of bliss that we have all known. Like the memories produced under the influence of LSD.

Kouhouesso smiled and took a drag of the joint. Africa exists, he said. Before him, three children had died, three sons mourned when in fact they were the same spirit returned to the same womb. He was the first to have lived because the preceding child, finally recognised for what he was, had been buried with the proper funeral rites. On his grave, near his head, the shaman had planted a special stake around which were woven carefully chosen leaves. The abiku would no longer trouble the family. Nine months later, Kouhouesso was born. His name meant 'The stake of Death has been planted'. He had been born to carry this name, a name he had lived up to by surviving beyond the age of seven, when the abiku could still make an appearance, and by remaining alive all the years since then.

After him, a girl was born, who had also survived and

whose name was Losoko, which meant 'We have thrown away the hoe'—the hoe used for digging graves. She had stayed in their homeland and they sometimes shared photos on Facebook. And last of all, a brother, who had also survived and who worked on construction sites in South Africa. His name was Orukotan, 'There are no more names left'.

It was a powerful name, which banished the abiku children forever, but also any other children, and so the mother stopped giving birth. And the father died quite quickly of septicaemia.

'I was born after a child died, too,' said Solange. If they had performed funeral rites in the village, if they had managed to cover up the whole business with stakes, hoes and unpronounceable names, if they had gathered around the little dead body and behaved like Zulus, would their devastation have been less brutal? Would they perhaps have managed to speak to each other? To get together with a little bit of joy at Christmas? She was about to reach for the photograph on the bookshelf when Kouhouesso pronounced solemnly, 'You're a sort of abiku of the north. Perhaps that's what appealed to me.'

So she appealed to him. He had said it: 'appealed to me'. And just as she was going to divulge the name of her brother (an ordinary name, and so French), just as she was about tell him a tiny portion of all her huge secrets, just as, in their lovers' intimacy, on the eve of their departure, in the intimacy of the shared joint, she was about to reveal the tiniest portion of what they never talked about, or at least not yet—about the past, families, perhaps her son, perhaps the future—just as she was going to speak, he kissed her passionately and they made love again.

BUSINESS CLASS

He hated psychological claptrap. Not all the inventions from the north were to be rejected, of course—medicine and science were especially welcome—but the only worthwhile psychology was that used with dreams, taboos and deep-seated forces. As an actor, he had always rejected psychological motivation, all the fuss around Coppola's directions, to Brando, Hopper or Sheen—each one more drugged and hopeless than the other, in any case. He was interested in phenomena connected with the collective unconscious, and all forms of non-verbal communication; but the individual unconscious left him cold. In *Heart of Darkness* there is not *one single* psychological explanation: just facts, actions, consequences. One driving force: inordinate greed. One type of conduct: brutality. One result: hatred.

It's up to the audience to work out what the emotions are, if that's what they're after. As director, he would leave it to the actors and actresses to delve into the depths of their souls, but in silence, for God's sake.

She was in love with a man whose name was The Stake of Death Has Been Planted. She tried to get used to this idea. And she loved it that he explained things to her, that he cared enough to explain things to her. If he spoke to her it meant he loved her.

On the plane he was happy. He wanted to see Paris again, the historical buildings. He never imagined he'd have so many interviews lined up. He stretched out his long legs in his spacious seat; she held his hand between the wide armrests; he would have happily smoked a cigar. They ordered champagne, vodka frappés and truffle canapés. Air France was still Air France, goddamn it. He hardly ever swore, or only as a joke. He even made a point of speaking a more polished French than was necessary, as if he felt responsible for the respectable behaviour of every African in the world. In the business-class cabin of flight AF066 to Paris, in which only a gentle rumbling could be felt at take-off—here, in the luxury of the skies, flying over the northern snow, it was the stewardesses he spoke to. He and Solange had champagne, beauty, and the pleasure of being looked at, recognised, and of being the subject of no end of attention, and of clearly being the most glamorous couple in the plane (538 passengers).

Yes, he wanted to see Paris again, the historical buildings. And he was happy about all the appointments. When he had managed to emigrate, Paris had seemed more familiar to him than his birth country. Cameroon was dysfunctional, but he wasn't. He recognised everything. The culture, the language; France had been in his blood since childhood: he'd recited Molière and Racine and fallen desperately in love with his French teacher (he didn't elaborate on this chapter of his life). His whole being was shaped by the idea of structure that characterised the French people, by the structures of the French language. He had seen Paris a thousand times. The sharpness of the avenues, cut sheer between the façades of the buildings, the pavements, the pedestrian crossings, the number of shop windows, the shiny cars, the efficient Métro system: he knew it all. That's where he came from, where he felt at home, in that smooth, open, sparkling world.

In the beginning, he had managed to rent an apartment thanks to a director who had taken on the lease in his name. Kouhouesso had wanted to become French; his application had been rejected. He only had a temporary visa but he had a Mercedes, one of the beautiful vintage models he loved. He was performing in a Chekhov play in Avignon and had driven all the way down, following the Rhône: his car was dirty and he didn't want to arrive filthy at the Avignon Festival. He found a garage where they washed cars by hand and had just paid, including the tips, and was doing a final inspection when a guy pulled up and held out his keys: 'When you've finished that one, do mine.'

It was nothing, just one incident. But, as an *African*, and in general, he decided that France could go to hell, and he became Canadian.

They had just flown over a big chunk of Canada. Through the plane window, they could see the polar icecap, re-formed for winter, passing by below. Canada was a last resort. He said it was his 'only unhappy love affair': Canada had made him one of its own, but he wasn't Canadian.

She waited a while and then said that Paris was her city, that she would love to show him the street in the Charonne neighbourhood where she used to rent a room, the Amandiers Theatre, her friends Daniel and Lætitia, and then, on the way to Lisbon, the Basque Country; it was Christmas, after all, her family was there…He had signalled to the stewardess for some more *champagne* (with a Parisian accent) and raised his glass to her: 'Cheers! To *Heart of Darkness*.'

She made a scene right there, in business class, over the Arctic Circle. For months, all she had heard about was his film, couldn't he possibly, even for two minutes, show some interest in what she had to say? Or was he *congenitally* incapable of listening to her?

The glaciers slid past, impassive. There was the tip of Greenland. He apologised. 'There are doors I need to knock on in Paris, for the film. When I've finished, I'll be less preoccupied.'

She concluded that he was being more sincere than rude. A film—pre-production, the shoot, the editing, post-production, distribution—a year. She would wait.

HOW COULD I KEEP MY WITS ABOUT ME

As always, there were exquisite flower arrangements at the little studio Daniel and Lætitia had lent them and, wonder of wonders, a little Christmas tree. She pulled out the sofa bed and Kouhouesso's long body completely filled the tiny attic room. They got up at dusk, it was only five o'clock, winter over the roofs of Paris. In the kitchen area, under the eaves, he had to bend over so he wouldn't bump his head. She taught him the expression 'ye olde', for the exposed beams, part of the charm of the Marais. She called a contact for some weed, and they got some good wine delivered. He had hardly listened to his messages, or checked his emails; he was, it seemed, *on holidays* for the first time since she'd met him.

He had a shower the way he usually did: with a plastic supermarket bag on his head. Even at specialist hairdressers he'd never found a big enough shower cap. He sat in front of the mirror for a long time, twisting his hair, then tied the loops at the back of his neck. She watched him; it reminded her of when she was a little girl, watching her father shaving carefully.

They made love swiftly, in one burst. It took their breath away. She would have given ten years of her life for those few minutes. It was madness. An illness.

She could have stayed there, absolutely self-contained beneath the roofs, until the end of the world, but he wanted to go out for dinner. Men always have to eat, go out. He spoke to her in *camfranglais*: '*Whatever, whatever, let's Johnnie there?*'—Johnnie Walker, the whisky of walkers. She laughed and they set off at a clip towards Bastille. They stopped at Zadig & Voltaire; the salesgirls made a beeline for them. She bought him a sea-green fine cashmere jumper. The floodlit city was brighter than in daylight; seen from a satellite, Paris must have been twinkling like a Christmas tree.

'Solange.' He was calling her. The roar of the traffic on the square was so loud that he'd had to say those syllables, *Sol-ange*, the *an-* like the *am* in *champagne*. She felt effervescent. Her, and no one else: Solange. She was becoming real. She existed, out of all the women here on this particular section of the Earth that had witnessed the world changing— 'Solange!' Near the canal, he pointed to the entrance of the amusement park, the statue of the black man with the huge mouth who was collecting tickets on his butler's tray.

She in turn pointed to the Spirit of Freedom on top of the column: the angel holding aloft broken chains. He called her idealistic and 'my little Frenchwoman'. And he kissed her.

Looking back, that short walk in Paris was perhaps the happiest moment of her life. After that sublime moment, everything was a letdown, a dangerous drifting off course.

People looked at them. They were beautiful, certainly, like they were on the plane, but there was something else. They were political. She who never used that word savoured the provocation of walking arm in arm with him. Nothing much: a minute disturbance of the atmosphere, a slight hesitation as passers-by looked at them: a black person and a white person. Together. Beautiful and wealthy and happy. And she noticed that there was always a touch of envy, or complicity, a sort of reverse aggression, in the way they were looked at, as if they were a couple of famous criminals, doomed but dashing romantics, the Bonnie and Clyde of Humanity's Happiness. Solange and Kouhouesso, pray for us.

She cuddled him. 'We're making quite an impression.'

'That's normal,' he chuckled. 'We're stars.'

Paris was whirling around them; they were being swept up from the square, *Comment ne pas perdre la tête, serrée dans des bras audacieux?*[1]

---

1 'Locked in such a bold embrace, how could I keep my wits about me?' From a popular French song, 'Mon Amant de Saint-Jean', written by Léon Agel in 1942, interpreted by many singers, including Edith Piaf and Patrick Bruel.

At the end of the canal, at Boulevard Richard-Lenoir, she lost him for a moment. He had gone into a chemist and was standing, tall and impossible to miss, at the hair products counter: in front of the Carissa-brand shea butter, argan conditioner for split ends. As a shocked salesgirl looked on, he opened a bottle and got her to smell it. That was it. Frankincense. Myrrh and gold, the Magi. She went weak at the knees, reached for the back of his neck, and kissed him. 'I can only find it in France,' he said. Did he jump on a plane as soon as he ran out? Did he seduce a French girl whenever he had none left? The salesgirl, a metre from them, was standing stock-still, fascinated. He paid the paltry amount on his American Express card and they walked out with a bag full of bottles.

They hailed a taxi and had dinner at the Terminus Nord. She would have liked to show him around the Goutte d'Or, but he wasn't keen on seeing those African neighbourhoods, no taste for such exoticism, no *ndolè*[2], no peanut chicken: he wanted foie gras and fig jam, oysters, sea snails, a grilled sole and some Pouilly-Fuissé.

They chatted; she felt hot; the wine and the jetlag and something about Christmas had gone to her cheeks. She mentioned Clèves, her southern Christmases, the absence of snow, the occasional red wind that deposited sand on the windows, sand that her mother claimed came from the Sahara. But she'd lost him already. She knew him well

---

2   A Cameroonian dish of stewed nuts, *ndoleh* leaves and fish or beef.

enough: when she spoke about herself, he preferred her stories that intersected with the big picture: what it meant to be Basque, for example; her experience of France, of a particular school, of secular education; the astonishing refusal by the French republic to use the word 'race'. Although she was thinking about her son, she spoke about Brice, her West Indian lover, and how she had not noticed that he was black.

Kouhouesso shrugged. She was adamant. At the time, she had focused on other aspects of Brice. But talking Congo and Conrad non-stop, she was bound to end up with a flushed face.

He rubbed his eyes with the flat of his hands.

'You saw the look the salesgirl gave me.' It was a statement, not a question.

'Anyone opening bottles of Carissa without indicating whether they intended buying them would get a dirty look,' she pleaded.

'What gave her the right to think that I wouldn't buy some?'

She let it go; it was useless; he did not want to listen. Exhaustion prowled round them like a coyote.

But she started in again: 'Brice himself never spoke about his colour.'

He cut her off: 'You're after a certificate. A certificate of non-racism. In fact, you're only sleeping with me as a way of obtaining it.'

She shook her head vigorously, like a horse, a wounded

horse. She muttered the word *paranoia.*

He pressed his palms against his eyes, then opened them, calmer now. 'All those charming salesgirls, they remind me of those American girls, rushing up to say hello and goodbye and pretending that they're colour blind. It's important to them that they pass the test. Listen. You're not that sort of petty person. But if you didn't notice Brice's colour, that just goes to show how *repressed* you are.'

The bastard, he had undergone analysis, too. Jungian, he told her. In Palo Alto, return trip twice a week in his Mercedes Coupé.

'I'm not repressing anything,' she protested.

'I can't remember who said: *to be Jewish is to ask oneself what it means to be Jewish.* I ask myself what it means to be black. Yet everyone seems to know. When you're black, others see it all the time. And who is the other? It's me. The role I'm expected to play.'

She didn't want to talk about Jews. Or black people, for that matter. Or others. She wanted to speak about them and about the rest of their trip and about Lisbon or not Lisbon and about children.

They finished off the seafood. The sole arrived; he sent it back—overcooked. Another sole arrived—perfect. He asked her to help him remove the bones, since she was born a fisherman's granddaughter. She was touched that he remembered. He looked at her kindly. He knew just how brittle truth was. Whether they liked it or not, *whatever, whatever*, they inherited centuries of cut-off hands, of whippings and deportation. And he didn't believe that love was stronger than death; that was only good for Walt Disney. No, they couldn't love each other inside a bubble or under Mary Poppins' umbrella.

Love. That was the first time he had said the word. The first time he had conjugated the verb to love with them as the subject.

She paid the bill; she had received a big cheque from Warner, and they were on her turf. Besides, they never went out in Los Angeles.

I HAVE TWO LOVES

It was the Christmas–New Year break and yet he had a series of meetings, one that day at Studio Canal, and on the 31st with Why Not. And Vincent Cassel's name kept popping up, like magic. Cassel…Cassel…he was the man of the moment.

She looked up the train timetables to Clèves (and perhaps to Lisbon) and booked two first-class TGV tickets for the following day, a three-day getaway. Kouhouesso was in a delightful mood. Naked under ye olde beams, he sang, wiggling an imaginary belt of bananas around his waist:

I have two loves, two you, two you,
Paris and my native land
Both forever, two you, two you,

My heart is at their command
Hollywood is sublime
But no one can deny
It hits me every time
Paris makes me high

He told her about Josephine Baker, about Katherine Durham, about Miriam Makeba. He showed her a Makeba concert on YouTube, in Stockholm in '66. She was wearing a leopard-skin sheath dress. 'Isn't that playing the racists' game, wrapping yourself in an animal skin when you're black?' asked Solange. He explained to her how the leopard skin was a sign of royalty. The only female black stars at the time were American or Caribbean. He was waxing lyrical, shocked: how could she never have heard of Makeba? He put on 'Pata Pata' and took her hand to dance. He wanted to make a popular film, flashy, sexy, full of music and adventure, not a pretentious film, not a French film. He had a meeting with Boris from Formosa, who had already produced films in Africa.

She was surprised he hadn't asked her to go with him: she knew Boris from Formosa well. But it would appear that Kouhouesso had quite a past in Paris, a whole life and plenty of connections.

It was evening, she was waiting for him at the studio, the lights twinkling on the Christmas tree. They were expected for dinner at Daniel and Lætitia's. The minutes were ticking by. She had spent the afternoon with Rose, in a hurry to tell her about the *two you, two you* incident. 'Oh, he's so funny!' Rose said. 'You have to marry a man like that, my dear!' She looked at herself in the bathroom mirror. Were her breasts too small? And what about her belly? Her figure still perfect, a young girl's hips. It was time she told him about her son.

She called Rose. She called her mother, and her father, and her son. She called Daniel and Lætitia, to tell them they would be late. She saw his name come up on her screen, *Kouhouesso*. She answered straight away: they should start without him, he was extremely busy, Cassel was in Paris and he might be able to catch him in Belleville.

There was a full moon. The rotating beam from the lighthouse of the Eiffel Tower made the grey roofs wobble. If she drew their love in circles, he would take up the whole centre of her being, and she would be on the periphery of his orbit, like a little moon whose tides he would not be affected by and which would never eclipse his Big Idea.

*

At 10.15 p.m., in the taxi, he reprimanded her for having waited for him. 'People have dinner late in Paris,' she announced, as if it were some sort of local custom. He was excited, radiant. Cassel was keen to come on board. And he had some fresh ideas. Boris had sent him the transcript of a speech that Sarkozy had just made in Dakar. Kouhouesso was reading bits out loud and laughing with the taxi driver, who turned out to be from Brazzaville. He was coming out with lines, interspersed with extracts, holus bolus, from the speech, all in the voice of a character, the president of the African colony.

The tragedy for Africa is that the African Man has not become part of History. The African peasant, who for thousands of years has lived according to the seasons, whose ideal life is one in harmony with nature, knows only the eternal cycle of time, in tune with the endless repetition of the same gestures and the same words. In this apprehension of the world, where everything is forever beginning again, there is no place for either human adventure or for the idea of progress. 'Straight out of the nineteenth century,' Kouhouesso explained, continuing verbatim, merciless. *In this universe where nature rules, people avoid the anguish of History that torments modern man, but they remain static in the middle of an immutable order in which everything seems to be preordained. They can never launch into the future. It never occurs to them to leave behind repetition and to invent a new destiny for themselves. This is the very heart of the problem with Africa—with your permission, I speak as a friend of Africa.* 'No mention of mass graves. Not the lightest hint of insincerity. A discourse from before Leopold II's time.' *The problem with Africa is that it must stop repeating itself, stop forever looking back. It needs to free itself of the myth of the eternal return, realise that the golden age it is perpetually lamenting will never come, precisely because it has never existed. The problem with Africa is that it is living too much in a present that is nostalgic for the lost paradise of childhood.*

He was cutting and pasting on his phone, in the taxi, all the way to Daniel and Lætitia's. The taxi driver didn't say another word; the guy was more or less in a state of shock. Was it possible, for once, to speak about *something else*? It was 10.51 p.m. She sent a last text to Daniel, asking for the door code. They rang the bell, Daniel opened, and she said, 'Kouhouesso,' and Daniel said, 'Oh. Nice to meet you.' She knew the 'oh' was a faux pas.

*

In the taxi on the way back he was doing that thing of pressing his palms against his face, a gesture of anxiety, distraction and—she had learnt how to read him—despair.

Did she have to *alert* people? Of what? His height, all 190 centimetres? His spectacular beauty? His mass of hair? Was she the guilty party, for letting them be taken by surprise? For not having pronounced his tricky name earlier? For *being* with him?

'I'm supposed to get to know them but they make no effort to find out where I'm from.'

They were driving along by the Bois de Boulogne. The Moldavian taxi driver was not joining in.

'It's the opposite…They're curious, actually…They're afraid of asking you questions because they don't want to stigmatise you by asking you where you come from.'

'I'm not afraid of being asked where I come from. They see Paris as the centre of the world. The three Guineas and

Ghana, Niger and Nigeria, Zambia and Zimbabwe, it's all the same to them. And the Battle of Algiers, if they happen to remember it, was in the middle of nowhere.'

He retreated into his morass of anger, into the violence of bloody-minded History, rock-solid History. He was inside a time past, a present in the shape of a geodesic curve, which—here, in Paris—was relevant only to him. But she was in the taxi, and she wanted to be with him, together in that irreconcilable time.

She turned towards the huge black trees and told him she had a son. Who had chosen to live with her father, with whom he got along well—better than with her mother—and to whom she had sort of entrusted her son, let's say, soon after he was born. Her own father, she means, given that the alleged father of her child had disappeared, moved out, as soon as her belly began to show. She'd had him very young, too late for an abortion and *whatever, whatever* (she liked the expression), there we are.

Kouhouesso knew.

Knew what? That she'd had at least one child. Had he been reading the gossip columns? Had he Googled her? No (he lowered his voice in front of the Moldavian taxi driver): it was her areolas. They were brown. 'White women have pale areolas, unless they've given birth to a child.' She felt as if she were going back, in the taxi, not only to Clèves, but to the 1980s, when she heard and repeated all sorts of rubbish—that you can tell by looking at someone if they're not a virgin anymore and that boys with long fingers have long dicks. 'It's a hormonal fact,' Kouhouesso insisted. Who told him? How many white women had he slept with? Do black women's areolas go darker? Why was she always full of questions, and he wasn't?

THE PROBLEM WITH AFRICA

In the stairwell of the studio, he told her that he had a meeting the next morning. In a few hours' time. 'But the train,' she exclaimed. He looked surprised. Centrifugal energy scattered the Christmas tree, her parents, her son: if he was staying, she was staying in Paris. No, come on, she should go and see her family; he needed to stay for the film. They argued on the landing. She rummaged in her bag for the keys. They had had too much to drink; she would set the alarm for tomorrow morning, as planned, and they would leave, catch their fucking TGV. The neighbour appeared, wearing a furious look and a dressing-gown—here we go, she thought, we're going to end up down at the station for disturbance of the peace and breaking whichever law. But the neighbour took one look at Kouhouesso and beat a retreat.

She couldn't find the keys. In a hushed voice, Kouhouesso was cursing: he had back-to-back meetings, he had to be *in top form*. The keys had slipped into the lining of her bag.

He sat at his laptop. The light annoyed her. When he finally came to bed, he lay still and fell asleep straightaway. She got up and felt in his jacket. His passport was there, the little navy-blue Canadian booklet with the Commonwealth coat of arms on the front. Stealing it would be a way of making sure he couldn't leave again.

His first and last names took up two whole lines. Kouhouesso Fulgence Modeste Brejnev Victory Nwokam-Martin. He must be the only person in the world with a name like that. He had told her that his father was a communist sympathiser, which explained some of his name. And he had obviously dropped the French bit.

He looked so young in the photo, shorter dreadlocks, a sleepy look.

She put the passport back in his jacket. It would be hard to think of anything more contemptible than stealing a black person's papers.

The alarm went off at six o'clock. They got dressed, made coffee. Kouhouesso grabbed the keys off the table and carried her suitcase to the Gare Montparnasse.

So, there was no point in her meeting him in Lisbon. He wasn't certain he'd get there. Let's be realistic: neither of them was very family-oriented. She had to exchange his return ticket to Los Angeles for an open return ticket; only she could do it, as she was the one who had made the initial transaction. So, he would reimburse her the difference—in any case, the expense would be part of pre-production.

She sat in seat number fifteen in carriage number one. He carried her suitcase on board. When he stepped back onto the platform, she felt the train wobble and lean to one side. She focused on breathing to stay calm. He placed his hand flat against the window, his red palm, against which she placed hers, smaller, cold from the glass—did their fate lines and love lines meet up and point towards the same horizon of creased skin? She pressed her mouth to the glass, but he didn't. He smiled, shadows under his eyes; the condensation formed a crown around his head.

With the first lurch, the condensation evaporated. The outline of their hands remained, ghostly, and once it had faded she had the feeling that she would never see him again, that she should never return to her family, that she should stay with him, not relinquish him, but follow her desire, forever. The train tore her from him; France rose and fell in the window labelled security glass. After Poitiers, she sent him a text, once there was nothing more she could do: 'I miss you.' He replied: 'Me too.'

Whatever, whatever, the train rolled on, France was flat, green and watery, time was passing at 300 kilometres per hour and she fell asleep after the 'Me too'. All of a sudden France had become forested. On the station platform, everyone was there: her father, her mother, her son. They had aged; her son had got even fatter. 'You came by yourself?' She had prepared the ground for Kouhouesso; she had told them his name. All that, and now this. They were on their way to Clèves in the car, still another hour to go.

She started drinking straightaway, in front of the twinkling Christmas tree. Her father handed her a whisky: come on, a bit of festive spirit; he took it right out of his ex-wife's sideboard as if they had never been divorced. No news since the text message at Poitiers. Where was he? What was he doing? Her mother insisted on seeing what he looked like, this boyfriend-who-did-not-come. 'He had a meeting with Vincent Cassel,' Solange boasted. She showed a photo of Kouhouesso. 'Solange always comes up with real doozies,' said her mother, and her father pretended to be a cannibal: 'I hooooope he's not going to eeeeeat you.'

This man, who could not look at a black person without taking on a ghetto accent, this man, who—she usually forgot—was born in Dakar like Ségolène Royal and had spent the first four years of his life there, this man said, 'Sarkozy is such an idiot' when they put on the news before dinner.

Her mother had cooked a fattened rooster. Solange's son was getting fatter and fatter, and, she had to admit, more and more ugly. He looked horribly like their old neighbour. 'Do you remember Senegal, Dad?' It was the first time she had asked him. He could only remember one thing: the Harmattan, the dry wind from the Sahara: dust, his burning throat, blood dripping onto his little smock because he was laughing with a friend and his chapped lips split, *crack*. 'So, it's a type of foehn,' her mother said. 'We have the same sort of wind here.'

She had brought her mother some Poison perfume and a signed photograph of George (her mother collected them). Some whisky for her father (bought duty free, along with the perfume). For her son, the very first iPhone and the latest iPod. And, for all three of them, she had filled in her customary vouchers: a return trip to Los Angeles, valid for the following year. Her father remembered the good old days when he got discount flights on Air Inter. All of a sudden, a text message: 'Send me your address.' He must mean her address here, in Clèves. Was he planning on coming? Tomorrow? Text message silence. Her dinner was whisky.

She went upstairs while her mother was getting out the Yule log. The dwarf ice skaters on the icing reminded her of Christmas at Jessie's. Galaxies from here. In her room, the Playmobil pieces were in the same place she had left them a year ago. Her mother mustn't have opened the shutters since then; lit by a bulb in the ceiling, it was the bedroom of a girl who had disappeared. She pulled apart the Playmobil pieces; last Christmas she had piled them up, like an orgy, their little hooks grabbing imaginary genitals, girls and boys, boys and boys, girls and girls, along with the swimming pool, the campervan, and a horse. What was going on in her mind a year ago? There was really no point asking the question. She had no memory of herself. Back then, she was already waiting for Kouhouesso, without knowing it, suffering less. She was still waiting for the future, just as she had been here in Clèves when she was fifteen, but back then the immediate future appeared in the form of a baby, surprise, surprise. A baby who, twenty years later, could barely speak. But that was understandable.

She would have liked to tell Kouhouesso her stories. *Pour her heart out.* In her childhood bedroom, under the light bulb with the rattan lampshade, she started whispering to him. She had had a child very young, like African girls did. In *Voici* magazine, just before she left for Hollywood, they had even written that her son was eighteen; it was all lies. She should have sued them. 'Solange!' Her mother was calling from downstairs, the same sound as when she was young. She opened the shutters, and rolled a joint. The garden was in darkness; behind the cypress trees, she could see the lights on in the house where Rose's parents lived. 'Solaaange!' The same summons. She carefully lined up all the Playmobil pieces along an imaginary pathway, then downed the whisky and knocked them into the campervan. She would find them again in the same spot in a year's time. No, she wouldn't come back. Or just with him. 'Solaaange!' She fiddled with the Playmobil so that she wouldn't die. So that something would keep happening in that bedroom. Otherwise the Playmobil pieces would outlive her. Those things are indestructible. She left her glass, the size of a jacuzzi, in the middle of the toy swimming pool. She noticed that Playmobil people were all white.

Her son hadn't moved from the couch. A plate with dwarves on it was lying on the floor. Something about those dwarves annoyed her. She was drunk. No, it was the joint. She raised her head and saw Kouhouesso. No, her father. She was an idiot. He was opening a bottle of his precious Saint-Émilion. The same attitude, shoulders back, neck held high, cigarette in his mouth. And the voice, that's what it was. The dictatorial solemnity. To pronounce whatever nonsense, as well. Older now, obviously. And white-haired. And bald: that was the funniest bit. But the same: same nose, same forehead, same slightly Chinese eyes.

The next morning—no, it was midday—the next day, she had no memory of her son leaving. Did her father drive him? Even though he was drunk? Her mother told her that a truck had come by, yes, a truck, not the postman, but a delivery man—with a FedEx package for her, signed for by the neighbour because the whole house was asleep. Her daughter obviously didn't do things the way everyone else did. The package made a rattling sound when she shook it.

It was a box of strange brownish-red fruit, the size of plums, as hard as walnuts. And there was a letter, or rather a scrawled note. It was the first time she'd seen his handwriting. 'Some kola nuts from the Château-Rouge market. *Ciao ma belle.*'

What did that mean, *ciao ma belle*? If she imagined him saying it, it was tender, macho in a nice way. If she just read it, for what it was, it was a farewell. Was that a metaphor, sending nuts? She was going mad. He had told her how much he was addicted to kolas as a child; she had never heard of them. Full of caffeine. In West Africa, everyone gives them as presents, as a sign of friendship, of welcome—when you're having drinks, whatever. She tried to peel them. She imagined his supple fingers stripping off the thick membrane. Fancy him remembering their conversation, paying that much attention—inside there was an ivory-coloured puzzle, pieces that fitted together perfectly, joined in order to be separated, shared. You could see it as a symbol, a thing cut in two; each person keeps a piece. It was surprisingly bitter for a friendship nut. And it made her fingers and teeth all red. She scrubbed them carefully.

She might as well head off on a bike ride along the river. A big sweater and old running pants. The cottonwool sky and the Nive River in winter, running high and silently beneath the bare trees, its surface grey-brown. Herons, moorhens, and an intrepid cormorant drying itself in an oak, far from the sea.

She daydreamed about his childhood, what he had told her about it, on the nights when she managed to get him to leave the computer. The intoxication of his words, yes—she had that feeling of being filled up with him, and then of being tense again, anxious to be with him properly, worried about having the right response, the right facial expression—to the point where all she could remember of his stories of playing in Benue was his fear of the hippopotami, and the capture of a crocodile, like in a story from Kipling. Two childhoods from the same time but on two planets—no, the same planet but different coordinates. When she was in Grade 5, he was a courier for a Lebanese guy running a brothel. When she was watching *Children's Island*, he was going to the cinema for the first time: *The Miracles of Berna-dette*, film reels carted around by missionaries and projected onto a length of printed fabric, the plainest they could find. The apparition of the Virgin in the cave at Lourdes was interrupted by little aeroplanes, *Super-Constellation* printed in copperplate, and the young paralytic started to walk with the slogan *Long Live Air-Africa Foreign Aid*.

His open return ticket! She had to get on to it.

He had learned to read all by himself, not from the projections onto miraculous printed cloth but from the cases of beer the Lebanese guy was trafficking. Then an uncle had helped him to go to a Jesuit school in Douala. He had devoured their library. She, too, had learned to read by herself, with John and Betty books. What was the point? He had never shown any interest in her childhood—did he think he already knew about the childhood of white girls, the identical childhood as told in all the books and films? But what about *her* river, *her* summer, the surprising heat of temperate countries? And their dense forests? She would have censored her sexual exploits; she didn't feel he was ready to know what she was like as an adolescent, the little wild girl, the young cannibal.

She thought about her father who, once he had got over the shock of meeting Kouhouesso, and had spouted his racist clichés as if out of politeness, would have settled into the serious issues: the rapport between men, the glass of red, the exclusion of women, male jokes. Everything would have gone smoothly. In fact, they would have got on brilliantly. Her father had lost his son. Kouhouesso had lost his father when he was a child. It would have been a perfect arrangement, clean and tidy like the strips of kola-nut skin. They had in common a silent world, a tough, seductive world where they stood alone, defeated or triumphant, but alone. And they both had a Big Idea; she was not sure exactly how to describe her father's—something to do with planes, blue sky, a spin-off business, diverse markets. He scorned chasing the yield: he was a man of the moment, taking the plunge, all in one go, heading into the wind. His Big Idea had not taken off, no doubt because he had not worked out exactly what it was. But she remembered the look in his eyes, the look into the distance, the look into which you wanted to disappear. What Kouhouesso saw, over there in the Congo, was the enormousness, the richness, the depth of horizon across the rivers. That was the problem with Africa, all that unfulfilled hope, and she could no longer live without it.

PART III

SOLANGE, BEST WISHES

Two and a half months without any news. Two and a half months. Without any direct news, at least: Ted and the executive producer had heard. He was location scouting in Africa. He had called from Luanda. He had visited studios in Lagos with his assistant and the director of photography. He had called from Kinshasa. The Congo was complicated. The Armed Forces of the Democratic Republic of the Congo (FARDC) and the Presidential Protection Division (DPP). The North—Kivu; and the South—Kasai. The Ugandan and Rwandan armies. And over in Tshikapa there was a full-on epidemic of Ebola. He had to retreat to Brazzaville. Even in Brazzaville, it was chaos. George's agent was fed up with it. She stayed tuned to the news like never before, at least she tried to—the news from over there.

Recently, he'd been moving around south of Cameroon, near the border with Guinea; he had sent a fax from a town called Kribi. She was following him on her mobile tracking app. At the end of the fax, which the producer showed her, he had added a line, in French, by hand: 'Solange, best wishes.'

She was left with 'best wishes' just like she had been left with his kola nuts: inside the skin, a bittersweet taste that was better than nothing.

She had received her contract: the Intended, three scenes with Cassel, interior day, location of shoot to be determined, $23,000. Everyone was making some sort of salary sacrifice (except Jessie, apparently). Africa had drained the budget, swallowed it up. On the other hand, given the cheap cost of local labour, fitting out a boat on the spot ended up being cheaper than a boat in the studio. As for the river, the location scouting had come up with the Ntem, the Dja or the Lobe. They still had their work cut out with the choppers. If they stayed in Cameroon, the tracks were supposed to be accessible in the dry season; he was scouting for caves that would be four-wheel-drive accessible. But it was borderline for George, whose window of availability was right when the rainy season began.

So that was the bulletin to the yellow hills of Hollywood, the news filtering through, bits and pieces, in the stress of preparations, among the cross-purposes, both obtuse and obvious, the contradictory, conflicting interests, all in an attempt to come up with a film.

Olga had been recruited: from the mourning dress to the crew's uniforms, from the raffia sarongs to the brass leggings, it was a real costume film. Natsumi had been promoted to costume props and was already at work on the 'polished gold ring stuck in the lower lip', on the charms and amulets, the feathers, the ankle and wrist bracelets. The make-up artist was brushing up on scarification, tattoos and teeth filing.

It did her good to spend time with the girls during her long Los Angeles days. She worked on her mourning dress with Olga; they chose the material together on Pico Boulevard. A grey dimity cotton. Mother-of-pearl buttons. A double hem in pleated crepe, with a ruffle and a belt. Puff sleeves with lace cuffs. Period stockings. A real corset. Long underwear. What wasn't visible on the screen was also important—a corseted woman, an Intended stiffened by grief.

She had ended up acting in *ER*, three episodes in a row. The wife of a diplomat refuses to leave the hospital until she can determine the fate of her son. She starts living in the waiting room, in the corridors and the cafeteria, her YSL suit more and more crumpled, both noble and a nuisance, and a romance develops with Dr Barnett. Finally, an interesting role, and she could pay for her house in Bel Air. They were talking about a comeback for her in the next season.

Two and a half months. How long does it take for a relationship to break off? For an affair to unravel? Love deteriorated. Idiotic love, which stops you from living.

Desire, which is a form of hell. *Ciao ma belle. Best wishes.* In the *ER* studios, in the arms of Dr Barnett—she was with him everywhere. Playing a woman rescued from a fire—a telemovie about Los Angeles firemen, a fee and a role beneath her capabilities; the director knew it and made the most of it. And she couldn't take refuge in the hollow of his shoulders. Rose was virtual on Skype; George was filming or on Lake Como; Olga was not really a confidante—and all the others, competing actors and actresses, were out for her blood. Lloyd, a kind and professional agent, treated her with long-suffering sympathy, as if all he could do now was wait for the end, the end of a terrible illness, one of those horrifying tropical contact diseases.

But the film was going to happen: George's contract was signed. Lloyd looked enigmatic, like the person who predicts the exact date of plagues—locusts, ulcers, the annihilation of herds of animals, the descent into darkness.

A year earlier, she had committed to the next Chabrol film. In a fit of sensible behaviour, she turned up in France on the scheduled date and it was *during this very film shoot* that Kouhouesso had reappeared in Los Angeles, and was looking for her—yes, looking for her, so it seems—and by the time she arranged to return, he was no longer taking calls; then he replied too late. Desynchronisation. No dates, no meeting places, no peace of mind. 'It's hardly conveni-ent': the last sentence she was left with, the last text from Kouhouesso. The next meeting, the only scheduled date, the only commitment, was playing the Intended, towards the end of the shoot, in six months' time.

She couldn't wait that long.

*

Incredibly motionless. Unmoving. Immovable. Anchored. Watching films he has watched. Polanski and even Pollack. Listening to Leonard Cohen on a loop. Preparing her role as well. Only hearing conversations in which, through various convolutions, his name cropped up. Reading books he had read. Biographies of Conrad. The story 'The Forest', by Robert Walser, in the last book she'd seen in his hands: she read and reread 'The Forest', looking for clues, tracks, the map of Kouhouesso's brain, the shape of his thoughts, 'incredible images of worlds where the forest went on forever…'

She looked for Kribi on Google Earth: the forest extends to the sea, unless it's the river, a thread of river for every thread of tree root…and the trees continue, beyond the Equator, through Gabon, through the Congo, and up to the north of Zambia.

Her stomach all scrambled, her mind on fire. A tight thread linked her to him, over there, in his forest. In which unimaginable, dense vegetation? Or in which coastal bar with which girl, which Favour, which Lola? She remembered that slightly old-fashioned novel from her childhood, *Future Times Three*, by Barjavel. The Traveller journeys through time, but he has a little rip in his spacesuit. In his belly. He disembowels himself. His intestines stay in the past while his body returns to the present. Poor gutted chook. She was the traveller staying in one spot. And which seer could read her future, when her entrails were uncoiled in the labyrinth?

A MOMENT OF GLORY

She woke up over Mali, went back to sleep. She woke up over
Kano for the breakfast tray. The earth was bright orange. The
place names came up on the flight information screen. Above
Jos she saw a river and a huge dark triangle—she couldn't
tell whether it was a lake or a rocky mountain range. Then a
series of parallel grey lines, one after the other. Then clouds.
Suddenly Mount Cameroon, a red island in the white sea.
Then they began the descent into Douala. She couldn't see
anything, not the mangroves as promised in Google Earth,
nor the river heading into the sea. They landed in clouds.
Clouds of hot water. She took off her sweater. The clouds
were in the city, in the airport. It smelled like fuel, sewers
and sugar. Under the sign *If you are accosted by unauthorised
taxi drivers, call this number* were thirty taxi drivers, all asking,

'What's it like over there?' As if they were fans, she smiled and waved, aloof. She saw on the screen that there was a delay of six hours for her connecting flight to Yaoundé. The counter where she stood to make a complaint was so wet she thought someone had spilt a glass of water. 'Wait here,' advised the stewardess in a Cameroon Airlines *boubou*, 'and don't get in a taxi.' Was it dangerous? No, but with the traffic jams, she probably wouldn't make it back—the bridge was impassable at that time.

Nevertheless, she was not going to spend six hours here without seeing some of the city where he had spent his adolescence, the beach where he must have daydreamed, out on boats, cargo ships. As soon as she had left the shade of the airport, she coated herself in SPF50 sunscreen. She had studied the area on the satellite app and located the highway, as well as a path on the right to the sea. She dragged her hand luggage and the wheels made a noise on the worn-out asphalt. Lots of people were on foot like her, and, like her, dragging or pushing paraphernalia, but, unlike her, they were all black. Women with objects on their heads, including a Dell computer. Children with goats. Daring motorbike riders with three or four passengers who called out to her, 'What do they do over there?' And cars tooted at her. There was no footpath. The way to the beach was there, off to the right, an ochre dirt path. A woman was selling mangoes. The beach? It was more like the port down there. Wasn't it lucky that all these people spoke

French. This was Kouhouesso's country, this was his birth-place—to hell with Canada.

Soon a wheel broke and anyway it was awkward dragging the little suitcase. She put her passport and her money in a pocket and hid the case under some leaves she would later learn were called 'elephant ears'. Right then they looked to her more or less like the philodendrons in dentists' waiting rooms. The path was no longer yellow but brown, and soft; her sneakers subsided and she felt momentarily demoralised when her toes became immersed in black water. A plane took off right over her head; the air smelled of kerosene and flattened vegetables.

They reached the river she had seen on the satellite app—a sewer, unfortunately, lined with garbage, and foul-smelling. Giant ficus trees or other green things had grown into tangled creepers. You would need to be the size of a frog and have the same skills. The jungle must have grown back since the satellite image had been taken; she had heard about this phenomenon: in the same way objects become coated with limestone in petrified waterfalls, so tropical plants grow over abandoned bodies.

She still had four hours but she retraced her steps. Her suitcase was there, covered in bees and water droplets. At the edge of the highway, she bought a fizzy grapefruit drink. It was all they had on the little stall called Moments of Glory. They didn't have it in 'lite'. Four hundred CFA francs: something like half a euro. Without change, she left a five-hundred-franc note. Traffic jams. Heading to the airport, the traffic was fine. A taxi was two thousand francs (still no change). 'You're on Cameroon Airlines?' The driver laughed. 'Here we call them *Maybe Airways*. You haven't reached the end of your journey yet.'

In the haze, night fell in a colourless sky. There was a sea of sorts, flat and metallic, a distillery, lovers sitting on rocks. No beach, a coast without a seaside, a muddle of vegetable fibre and water. It was not clear where the land began and where the water ended or which bit was the river. At the Cameroon Airlines counter the stewardess told her that the flight had been brought forward: they were waiting for the white passenger. She had to slip through the luggage airlock, behind the counter, quickly, with ten other latecomers rushing along. The little green, orange and yellow plane, the colours of a parrot, was sitting on the runway; she and the others ran towards it.

She had handled things like a pro. She would tell Kouhouesso all about it. Tomorrow. Tomorrow she would see him. She mused on the fact that she had only thought about him occasionally: the exotic is a distraction.

THE STRAIGHT AND NARROW

Yaoundé, the Hilton, waiting for the car. The trip was ridiculous, but it was the assistant producer who had organised everything: as seen from Hollywood, Douala, Yaoundé and Kribi must have seemed like a game of Scrabble spread out on a table. She had already made enough of a fuss to come early; she kept her geographical reflections to herself.

Kouhouesso wasn't answering. Perhaps there was no network in the forest. The driver booked by the assistant producer was on his way from town. How did we manage before mobile phones? The four-wheel drive smelled of Landes pine fragrance; the air conditioner was on full. The town levelled out as the trees got taller, fewer and fewer houses and more and more trees, until there were only trees. You couldn't really call it a landscape. There was nothing to see beyond the edge of the road, beyond that first row of trees, like a sort of huge hedge. The word 'forest' itself was inadequate. This forest and the Landes forest were as different one from the other as, say, the Atlantic and Lake Como. It was a whole other concept, completely different raw materials: as much green as you could wish for, but fleshy, bulging. And the path was rough. There was no more asphalt; there were holes, bumps, ditches in the middle of the road. To her mind, this was not a road but a trench, a gorge. With plank bridges.

Nevertheless, *whatever, whatever,* bit by bit she was getting closer to him. She was undertaking the final section along the arc that still separated them.

The driver's name was Patricia; no, Patricien. He was half-Baka, right…The song on the radio, 'We've come up with the question, we haven't come up with the solution', had a Congolese beat to it. She was hungry, so they stopped. The village (ten huts, an antenna and a handwritten sign) was called Washington. A street seller in the blazing sun offered them Nokias and cassava. Patricien showed her—pardon, Madame Solange—how to peel the stick of cassava to remove the sickly sweet, white paste, which was downright disgusting. That's how typhoid epidemics started. So he told her. It was better to eat fried plantain banana. But, guess what, they didn't have any there.

She rubbed her hands with antiseptic gel and would have liked to clean her teeth. A fierce stinging in her arm. It was a *mout-mout* sandfly. 'It doesn't actually sting you,' said Patricien, hedging, 'it eats into you.' She sprayed herself with Special Tropical Insect Screen. Wouldn't the Special Equator version have been better? Her mobile rang: Kouhouesso? No, her mother, calling from Clèves. Was everything going well? At the sound of the village church bells—it was midday there, too—her belly clenched. Was Jessie right after all? Perhaps it really was physically intolerable to be in two places at the same time; was the planet taking revenge, as it rotated, for being split in two like that?

Going to the toilet was actually a problem. They found a hole in a hut. She still had a stomach-ache, half from nerves, half from cassava. She swallowed two capsules of Imodium with a warm fizzy drink. According to Patricien, they still had about four hours of driving. The idea was to go as far as the river, leave the four-wheel drive with a guard at Big-Poco, cross in dugout canoes with the cargo: fifty kilos of rice, a sack of salt and a big sack of yams—two days of supplies for the local crew—as well as twenty packs of mineral water for what was known as the white crew. Then they'd take another four-wheel drive, known as a 'bridge', waiting on the other side, to do the transhipment, and keep driving to Little-Poco.

They set off in the Scandinavian climate of the four-wheel drive. All of a sudden she received a text, the letters appeared as they bumped along the track. Kouhouesso. A text that had travelled via satellites to reach her here, in

Washington, in this desolate backwater, to land on top of the towering antenna, taller than the trees, to form magic words, words addressed to her:

'So, African girl?'

That was so like him. Nothing and then that; it was so like him.

She sent him a super smiley, with extra brackets, and crosses for kisses.

On second thought, she also sent a summary of her schedule, her arrival time, in four hours, at Little-Poco, did that suit him, where should they meet, was everything going well?

Trees were flashing past, yes, they were immensely tall trees flashing past. She had to lower her head to see the tops; the slit of sky above the track was like an upside-down river. But what did places and times matter; the world here and now was once again inhabited by one man alone.

*

Kouhouesso was not at the village. They got her a room at the Straight and Narrow hostel; she made a fuss: she wanted Kouhouesso's room. Where was the 'white' crew? They were all at Big-Poco. Yes, on the river. Jessie, Favour, Mr Kou and his assistant, and the director of photography, and the cameraman, and the soundman, and all the production technicians, the Nigerians, the Cameroonians, and even Olga: everyone. It was better to sleep at the hostel: there would be no more 'bridge' vehicles at that time of day. As for Mr Kou's room, he had taken the key.

She lay down on a bench covered in raffia, and someone brought her a foam mat and some sheets that smelled musty. There was no wifi. There was no running water. She did what she could for her upset stomach, using a bucket, even though she wasn't sure it was there for that purpose. She rang Kouhouesso—she had reception, but did he? She unfolded her portable mosquito net, but where to hang it from? The plaster roof was rotten; a nail would not have stayed in. She shut her eyes. She tried to breathe in the incredible humidity and she held back her tears, because if she cried, there and then, that would be the end of her; if she cried she would melt away entirely; if she opened her eyes she would empty out all the water inside her and the only thing left, like baby Kouhouesso, would be a little pile of powder, white powder.

THE BOTTOM OF THE COOKING POT
DOESN'T MIND THE HEAT

The manageress of the Straight and Narrow advised her not to go out alone. It was six in the evening. She had not noticed night falling—it was black. There were no street lights. At the end of the path she could make out the little red lamps of two bars across from each other, and somehow she could hear, through the humid air, muffled shouts and Congolese music, and everywhere there were insects, nocturnal birds, frogs and cane toads and God knows what other living creatures in the forest, screeching, whistling, *pings, beeps, drings,* like thousands of mobile phones ringing for no one among the dense trees.

She shared a warm beer with the manageress, Siphindile. A thousand francs, a second one, a third. She was bored, at seven o'clock in the black night, watching a French telemovie starring Mimie Mathy. Bored and anxious. So she told her everything: how Kouhouesso was never there, how he was always silent, to which Siphindile replied that the bottom of the cooking pot doesn't mind the heat. In short, the early morning fog never deters the pilgrim. Where's there's a will there's away. So she wanted him? She just had to apply herself.

The electricity cut out. Ten or so fellows turned up, some in green uniforms, others armed with machetes. There were a few girls as well, who looked as if they were used to this. The electricity came back on. She relaxed a little. Warmer and warmer beers disappeared into 37-degree bodies. In this humid, organic air, it was like breathing yourself. The line between oneself and the world was blurred, the lungs opened directly out of the chest, skin dissolved. Or else it was the alcohol, or the people. They spoke dialect, but not all the same one, so they frequently reverted to French. She was penetrating the walls of Babel: they were not talking about her, they were not plotting anything, they all had real lives here, worries, jokes, none of which was any of her business; it was both strange and reassuring. The neon lights were swaying, there was a second of shadow, the insects fell silent. The blinking of a giant eyelid. The light returned, along with the vibration of the insects, a parallel current.

She was hungry. Could someone tell her where there was a restaurant? By the light of a torch, Siphindile took her to a place where a woman had some fish. Everyone followed. Cooking in palm oil and chilli, the fish smelled good, all the fish—she had bought the whole basket. A plate? They gave her a plastic bag, thick enough to hold the juice if she made a little fold, like that. The others ate straight off the table. She didn't dare disinfect her hands in front of everyone. Hooray: a poacher armed with a machete found her a fork. She ordered more beers, the last from the warm refrigerator. The air was completely still, the only light came from the TV and from a scrap of moon up high. A girl asked her if she could take the fish heads for her children. And for dessert? They produced papayas; she bought all the papayas. Slowly and steadily, she was becoming the manageress, with an ease that both disturbed and reassured her; since she was feeding the village, no one was going to eat her.

Nigeria versus Burkina on the TV and couples were starting to get together. She left to sweat off the beer on her foam mattress, in the hot air from the fan, which stopped and started as the electricity went on and off. In the intermittent blare of the soccer match, she woke and fell back asleep on her own on-off timer. Later, there was a knock on the door. It was Siphindile. It would cost one hundred thousand francs for Kouhouesso to get back. Fortunately she had brought an envelope full of notes. Siphindile cut off a lock of Solange's hair and wrapped it in a scrap of rice bag. The deal would be done during the night. The electricity cut out for so long that the soccer fans headed off. It was only ten in the evening. There were shouts and the eerie crowing of roosters, *cock-a-doodle-doo*, in the middle of the night.

Later on, there was the sound of digging under her window. She looked through the louvres; it was daybreak. Siphindile and another woman were bent over what looked like a small grave. They had wrapped their heads in matching cloths and seemed to be praying: Millet's *The Angelus*. In the morning there was just the trace of disturbed soil beneath the window. Siphindile had left her a basin of water; she threw in a few chlorine tablets and washed as well as she could. The ground absorbed the water straight away, black outlines, evaporating. A red lizard gazed at her. Two girls were asleep in a fake leather couch under the awning. She could hear the TV, live from France. *The Price Is Right* was about to start.

Weirdly, it was already midday. She wandered into the village. Siphindile had pointed out a place, in the 'Paris-Soir' neighbourhood, where she could recharge her phone. The stall holder had a small generator and a multi-socket adaptor, a hundred francs per recharge. She left her iPhone with him, uneasy about it. The forest began immediately, right there, behind the huts; yesterday she had assumed that black wall was the night. Trees, giant grasses, the occasional flower. She kept looking up, towards the treetops; she remembered the forest behind her house, when she was little, how everything seemed huge. And the fairytale about the princess: she had scarcely set foot in the forbidden forest when she was swallowed up. There were clicking sounds, fleeting bird calls. Elegant, black-edged white butterflies, whose head and body were like an Yves Saint Laurent logo. She was being bombarded by small hard objects—were little monkeys high above throwing turds? Kola nuts? That would be just great.

Her iPhone worked again, the stall holder was patting her phone with pride and awe, exactly the way her son had at Christmas. 2008. In the jungle. No messages.

All the Toyota vehicles were in the 'Manhattan' neighbourhood, parked crookedly in hollows and on mounds. Kouhouesso had come back. She got a lift to his hut. A guard under the palm-leaf verandah told her that Mr Kou was sleeping. He was there, on the other side of that bamboo-and-dried-mud wall, right there. She didn't dare disturb him. Children were coming home from school, immaculate uniforms and thongs on their feet, holding large leaves like umbrellas over their heads; they looked like little trees in motion, heading in single file towards a forested future.

Even Olga wasn't answering; she must have been sleeping in one of those huts. And Jessie? And where was Favour staying?

Back at Siphindile's there was nothing to eat but sticks of cassava and tins of sardines, two thousand francs each; but if she would like, there was a magnificent fresh rooster, for thirty thousand, only its heart and genital organs missing. They could grill it for her on the spot. She declined.

INCREDIBLE IMAGES OF WORLDS WHERE THE FOREST WENT ON FOREVER

She had taken some care choosing her outfit, a Vanessa Bruno summer dress. But she was too hot in it; silk is suffocating. In the shade inside his hut, standing erect like a king from ancient times, Kouhouesso was lean, smouldering, his eyes blazing. He greeted her with a peck on the cheek. He no longer smelled of incense but of the same vegetable, sugary, slightly musty smell that she already detected on herself. He told her that he was coming out of a 'little bout of malaria'. She was taking her Lariam, wasn't she? Her naturopath in Bel Air had prescribed her some quinine essential oil, but she didn't want to induce prophylaxis.

She stayed silent, feeling like the twenty-fifth wife, too little too late, coming to beg for an audience. Why didn't he embrace her? Why, after more than three months, didn't he jump all over her? He looked tired and was talking as if it were only yesterday that he had left her on the platform at the Gare Montparnasse in the cold fog of the Paris winter. The scenes in the forest were not working well. He had sacked the director of photography—Marco was no longer there?—and taken on the one Terrence Malick used; at least he'd know how to deal with the shadows and the green. Marco was threatening legal action, the producer in Hollywood was kicking up a fuss, and a camera had been stolen, as well as a video assist monitor and even some easy rigs—a little bit of everything had disappeared. They had found the camera in the Kribi TV shop; he'd had to buy it back at the American price. Why didn't she go and wait for him at Poco-Beach: it would be much more peaceful, a beautiful spot. Jessie and the Americans were staying there, as well as Favour, in custom-built lodges, electricity, bathrooms, coconut palms. She would be much better off there than at Little-Poco.

She hadn't come for the peace; she had come to see him. It would be difficult: he was working and moving around all the time, the boat still at Kribi, the sets in the forest, the sound production limping along. Water was a huge issue. Jessie had been sick, a catastrophe. She couldn't care less about Jessie. She moved towards him. He lay down on top of her, pulled up her dress. His mattress was damp, too. She abandoned herself, but him, what about him? She put her arms around him, hugged him. Where was he? In which Africa? When she opened her eyes again, he was smiling at her kindly. It seemed more like politeness than love.

Out the front of the Straight and Narrow, a woman was waiting for her, the woman from the night before, the one who was digging under her window. 'Five thousand,' said the woman. She didn't understand. 'Your bush husband back: five thousand.' Solange walked around her in silence. The woman grabbed her by the arm; the contact was uncannily cold. 'Five thousand.' She had already paid, and he would have ended up coming back to the village anyway. The woman made a strange cutting gesture in the air; in another world, in another context, it might have been a backhand in tennis, or a box cutter across the throat.

*

She was hot in the dugout canoe. The paddle dipped into the water as if into oil; the birds themselves fell silent. This heat was senseless; she could not stop herself from opening her mouth, but the air outside was much hotter than the inside of her body. Kouhouesso shut his eyes as if they were louvre windows, and the bare-chested oarsman wouldn't stop splashing himself with water. He paddled the heat, he stirred up the river and the sky, he liquefied in the mirages. The sheet of water was riffled by waves carrying the sound of voices, blasts, strange sounds coming from nowhere. The vibrations made their way into Solange's body. She had visions of the house in Malibu, the Mediterranean shade, the white-tiled bathroom, the sea generating currents of fresh air. That was yesterday, that was before. She would have liked to contemplate the forest, have the wisdom of painters and ecologists, but this flickering green and orange Africa was just one more problem. Not a single one of these trees explained Kouhouesso. They just amounted to one more enigma pitted against her, impenetrable, dangerous, a non-human kingdom, the manifestation of a power that was reduced to sawdust elsewhere.

Far ahead they could glimpse the construction site. Bulldozers were preparing the ground beside the river bank. Workers were laying rails, their shoulders dripping with sweat in the blazing sun. Kouhouesso wanted a tracking shot of the arrival of the boat. The uprooted mangrove trees looked like giant dead spiders, their legs in the air. They were clearing them out: mangrove trees were no use. The kapok trees were chopped into pieces for making kapok fibre and plywood. The occasional mahogany trees were sold as logs. She was learning vocabulary. There were a lot of trees without names, growing far from the French language: the *bibinga*, said the oarsman as they skirted the monumental trees. The *zoubé*, the *ekan*, the *alep*, the *okongbekui*. The graft hadn't taken: it was impossible to transplant French onto those fantastic forms, those voluminous roots, those magnificent verticals. Except for that one, tall and curved, bright green, luxuriant: rattan, neither a chair nor a table, but living rattan that thrust its palms into the water. Here they said *nlông*. And Freeboy, one of the Pygmy guides, used different syllables again for the same trees; it seemed as if there were as many names for a single tree as there were growth rings. The chainsaw sliced: *tchick tchick*. Then more slowly: *ebony*. It would end up in planks all the same. The Pygmies were the ones who stacked them.

Olga was there. It would have been a pleasure to see her again if Olga had been in the mood. But the blowpipes *made in China* had got lost between Shanghai and Douala. The arrows had got there safely, but Olga had been thrown by the behaviour of the customs officers at Douala. At first the blowpipes were regarded as weapons of mass destruction, and their container was held up; then they had never arrived; then the parcel was definitely there, but it wasn't a parcel of blowpipes; in any case she had to pay through the nose to get them cleared. Olga had decided to commission a local artisan to make two hundred blowpipes out of softwood; after all, there was no shortage of wood. On the other hand, around there they only knew how to make machetes and assegais; she had to do drawings and calculate the right dimensions. One by one, the local artisan made them. His name was Ignatius; he was up to one hundred and eighty. The whole village was in training, the two hundred extras, almost all the men, and the women when they didn't have something better to do. There were plastic arrows all over the ground, everywhere.

Solange was sitting in the shade of a frangipani tree, on a chair someone had brought there for her. She was sprinkling herself with a spray bottle of water. The legs of the chair were sinking into the ground. It was like a long siesta. She felt as if she was a germinating plant, her very cells proliferating. The ants were the only thing to watch out for; if an army of ants approached, she had to get out of their way. The ground was covered in dead leaves scattered with small beetles, and living creepers that she thought she could hear growing. She made herself shift around the shade's compass in little jolts, just to get the heat moving.

She had visions of Kouhouesso: he appeared in apparitions, flashes. He was *working*. He was *filming*. Lights. Camera. Action. She found it difficult to take, difficult to believe; she was on a film shoot without acting, not knowing what to do with her hands, her eyes, her body, her thoughts. Something was hovering, like air turning solid. Everything was vibrating in blocks of heat. Everything was dripping; the whole world was perspiring. Here at the Equator, the belt around the Earth, it was like an attack of shingles that was slowly going around, via her, Solange, on her chair. An illness which, once it had come full circle, would destroy her. The Special Tropical Insect Screen was useless: she scratched herself. Blisters. Kouhouesso seemed impervious to uncertainty; he had gone into another zone, into fiction. Occasionally she caught his eye; she would have liked to get up and kiss him in front of everyone, but by the end of the day the chair legs had left deep, narrow holes in the ever-present humus, like those left by spider crabs.

ONLY PEOPLE WITHOUT A VISION
RESORT TO REALITY

He hardly ever slept, at least hardly ever in the village. She kept hearing the four-wheel drives coming back from the river, from the caves, from Kribi. She called him but he didn't pick up; she knocked on the door of his hut. The guard stared into space, as still and wrinkled as a monitor lizard. 'It's me,' she said. No answer, but she heard the fan on the other side of the mud wall. 'It's me,' she said, louder. 'It's me, Solange.' Usually, he let her come in. The guard stared into the distance, towards the black wall of the forest.

Storms rumbled, passed by, without rain. A steady stream of Toyotas churned back and forth from Kribi: they needed water for the rain machine, bottled water. Jessie refused to perform in the storm scenes unless the machine ran on Évian. A thousand francs per bottle, imported through Douala. If a single drop of non-mineral water, even chlorinated water, found its way into Jessie's mouth (so his LA lawyer had warned), if a single drop of undrinkable local water contaminated him with amoebas or with God knows what African killer disease, the production crew and Kouhouesso would answer for it.

The rain machine, filled to the brim with Évian, was carried on board the boat by six locals and camouflaged with bits of metal sheeting at the back of the steam engine. Solange was also carried on board, and stashed in the hold, up to her waist. Lights. Fog machine. Action. The rain had to sweep over the river as well, bombard it with water. Everyone was soaked, the camera under a tarp, the cinematographer under an umbrella, and Jessie, half-naked and glistening, leaped around, wilder than wild, thrilled to be acting the fool. He opened his mouth wide, his gold lip-plate and all, and drank the thousand-franc water, the French water whose super-clear, super-pure alpine molecules combined with those of the brown river. The Company, as Kouhouesso called his production crew, was not going to be impressed. What sort of return could you expect from a business that threw thousand-dollar banknotes in the water? Why not film under a shower of champagne?

Later, the boat reached the shore in silence. The Hollywood rain had stopped. Kouhouesso was pleased; his scene was a wrap. Tomorrow they would shoot the rain of arrows:

under the orders of the assistant director, two hundred extras would each take aim five times. And, once the rails were finally laid, the tracking shot. Favour would appear, the Witch, the Creature in Brass Leggings. But right now there was a noise. 'Cut!' said the soundman.

Music. Incredible music. Sounds of *pop-pop* and *peep-peep*, *chh-chh* and *clap-clap*, more and more high-pitched, then dropping into low notes. A tom-tom but muted, mellow, like an accent—Solange thought she heard Kouhouesso's voice murmuring on the river from all directions. It was a Pygmy welcoming party. Well, no one was sure; no one knew if the Pygmy girls were doing it specially for them, but they looked at home there: twelve- or thirteen-year-olds completely naked, with little pointed breasts, standing in the brown water up to their waists, beating it with the flats of their hands, in unison. An elemental harmony, a skill so dazzling it could render you sentimental.

'Roll camera, roll camera!' shouted Kouhouesso. Solange could tell that he was *seeing* it all: no costume drama, no period setting, the little naked Pygmies had been there forever, and Joseph Conrad had seen them. But now they had stopped performing, all standing in the river as straight as the letter I. 'Music!' Kouhouesso yelled at them. 'Come on, what the hell—this time for Africa, girls, tom-tom!' They ran away, nut-brown naked buttocks leaping into the elephant-ear plants. It was over. Cut. It wouldn't make it into the film.

Kouhouesso jumped onto the bank and smashed his fist into the knotted furrow of a tree. *Crack.* The whole boat fell silent. 'Perhaps they'll be there tomorrow,' Solange ventured from the hold, where she was suffering from a slight bout of river sickness. Kouhouesso stormed into the jungle.

It is not possible to storm into the jungle. A long prickly creeper had hooked onto the back of his clothes, around his shoulders, back, waist, and Freeboy was hacking away, at his feet as well, in among the roots, in the whatever-they're-called plants: *tchick* went the machete. He had tracked them down. The girls were there, alert and curious, ready to take to their heels. '*Atchia,*' said Freeboy. They replied, '*Atchia.*' One little hand on the pubic area. The other held out to her, Solange. What did they want—the bottle of Évian she had saved from the downpour? The boldest girl held it in both hands, opened it. They took turns to drink, as if it were nectar of the gods, then gave it back to Solange with the lid carefully screwed back on. (What disease, what parasites, did those little mouths, those little hands, those round bellies harbour?)

Later, at the Pygmy village, Freeboy and Kouhouesso spoke with the chief. He was genuinely small. One of the surprises in this world is that Pygmies are small: the validation of a cliché, the fusion of idea and fact. 'You say *Baka*, not Pygmy,' objected Patricien, half-Baka himself, and of medium height. He was getting agitated. Kouhouesso had just given the order for fifty flasks of Fighter whisky to be purchased immediately in Little-Poco: the price he had agreed with the girls for them to perform their concert again. 'That's enough to kill the whole village,' said Patricien to Solange. He took her back to Little-Poco, by canoe then four-wheel drive. Solange was extremely hot and had a headache. 'You have to drink some water,' Patricien said. But all the viruses in the world seemed to be concentrated in what was left of the water in the Évian bottle.

*

Solange had a fever. Was she imagining the tom-toms in the distance, or was the Pygmy village celebrating, with shots from those little plastic flasks whose dubious benefits she herself was enjoying—full of a golden beverage, very strong and very bad, but scorching, and which seemed to clear a passage in the humidity?

He came to find her that night. He needed her opinion. He showed her the rushes on his portable monitor. Those foolish girls had got dressed up for their concert, one in a David Beckham T-shirt, the other with a sort of Petit-Bateau child's sleep sack stretched to fit her. In the water, it looked like a kind of Miss Pygmy wet T-shirt competition. There was Kouhouesso's assistant, then Kouhouesso himself, then several black giants and a white giant (the soundman), the whole crew of the film boat came into the frame, trying to persuade the girls. Jessie was clacking his gold lip-plate like false teeth and terrifying the girls. They took their clothes off and patted the water timidly with the flats of their hands. *Ploppity-plop, plip, plip, chlap.* It was rubbish, unusable—and the way they stared at the camera the whole time: impossible. Kouhouesso had made a mistake. Even if he had caught it unrehearsed, what would he have done with it?

It was all for the best: that sort of self-indulgence gets cut in editing. Instead of documentary-style girls what he needed was his blowpipes scene. Only people without a vision resort to reality—that's what the Zulus say. Novels, films! The attack on the boat. The swarm of arrows. Jessie, bleeding. He was waving his hands around, miming, standing up: the firearms responding, Winchester and Martini-Henry rifles, *bang-bang*, 'as though the mist itself had screamed'. She was laughing: he was the film, he was the trees, he was the boat and the river all by himself, he was the arrow and the gun, the corpse and the annihilator.

They drank a few whisky flasks together, tearing them open with their teeth. They were silent. The heat and fatigue had caught up with them. 'Still, it's not the Congo,' she said. He had wanted to see Paris, the historical buildings; she wanted to see the Congo, crocodiles. 'Fortunately there are not many crocs in the Ntem anymore,' he said, smiling. He had seen the Congo. The boats rotting on the Pool Malebo. They would have spent the film shoot paying over and over again, sending soggy scraps of paper to the Company, on which receipts would be written, in biro, along the lines of 'Departure Authorisation Tax', signed by a guy armed with a Kalashnikov, who would answer to the name of One-Eye-Only or Leftie, followed eight days later by another tax for another military guy, followed by another piece of paper, until the official had passed his use-by date or been bumped off, replaced by another gang, higher charges, embargos, ransoms. And the boat would not have moved. Here, they only had to pay up occasionally, and to people with names.

'Still,' she persevered, sucking on her flask of Fighter, without really knowing what she was talking about. They were being attacked by buzzing creatures. He rolled the mosquito net around them and pointed the fan at the creases. In the clammy, scratchy cocoon, riddled with draughts, they made love. The electricity cut out. The electricity came back on. Later, the tin can that served as a bedside table seemed to move of its own accord and ring out like a bell: mice were squabbling over her health-food biscuits. Kouhouesso chased them away. When he moved she felt the disruption of the fan's breeze. In the shadowed room she could not see him: he really was the invisible man, black in the night, air in the breeze.

Towards dawn she thought she heard digging under her window again. She was frightened to go and look, or to wake Kouhouesso. She took a sleeping pill. Since Christmas—since, what would she call it, her departure—she could no longer sleep. Since the night of the Playmobil. As if all the alcohol she had drunk in Clèves that night was still in her bloodstream, keeping her in permanent jetlag, in a state of everlasting fatigue, as impenetrable as a forest.

When she woke up he was gone. And under the window the soil had been disturbed, as if the ground had been stripped, pale yellow, soft, a trail of moisture leading from it, disappearing under the trees. She thought of the witch, and wondered whether to take her a five-thousand-franc note.

UP TO HIS NECK IN IT

Vincent Cassel was there for ten days. Ten days to do all the Marlow scenes, three of which were in the caves with George, whenever he arrived. Olga was keeping her up to speed. So a wardrobe mistress was more important than she was—but what did she expect, other than this crush of people, crowded in chaotic accommodation, taking communal meals or otherwise, each of them with a task that more or less overlapped with someone else's, all more or less feverish and sick, but all straining towards that imaginary interface where a book becomes a film? Where Africa becomes a story? With as much exertion as a boa constrictor swallowing a large antelope, with knots and jolts, hiccups, obstructions…

Only the Pygmy people went naked. The two hundred Bantu extras refused to be filmed naked. Or even half-naked.

It was contagious. A kind of craze. What image did they want to present of black people? They were being treated as savages. Two hundred raffia sarongs designed by Olga and sewn in Morocco, with ornaments for the head, nose, arms and legs: no way. A delegation led by a certain Saint-Blaise demanded five thousand francs more per extra for them to strip down to their Bantu birthday suits. Kouhouesso laughed: seven euros more for each of them, a million CFA francs, two thousand dollars, it was nothing. Not even the cost of the sarongs. And he hadn't forgotten that he owed Solange money: she should make out an invoice and the Company would reimburse her.

Hollywood versus the jungle: for five thousand more— five tins of sardines, a bit of roast chicken, a witch's tip—two hundred villagers decorated in lucky charms showered the boat with arrows and 'the bush was swarming with human limbs in movement'. The scene worked incredibly well. Jessie in particular was magnificent: he died with unexpected dignity, lying in the blood as if on a crimson mantle, with a look that was 'extraordinary, profound, familiar'. *You were wild, Jessie, you were sublime, I love you.*

The black people from here were not like Kouhouesso. But, more especially, they were not like Jessie. Jessie was not like them. Of course (as Kouhouesso explained to her), there are African-Americans who want to become African. To be reunited with the Africa that was stolen from them. In general, the affair ends badly. Either they are too frightened ever to leave the Monrovia Sheraton, or else they are repatriated with dysentery. At worst, they end up as rastas in Addis Ababa, preaching that women have the mark of the devil, without ever giving up their American passports. There are infinitely more Africans who want to become American. Or, failing that, Canadian.

He took a drag on his cigarette and she had him back, the Kouhouesso who explained things to her, who unpacked them, who so royally shaped the world for her. They had celebrated Jessie's last day of filming until dawn, and Kouhouesso had come back with her to the Straight and Narrow. How had she coped without his tireless commentary? It was like being deprived of her own eyes. Her own hands, she thought, as she took his in hers. Of her own head on her own neck. Of her own soft, muted voice. She kissed him in the hollow beneath his Adam's apple. And she asked him if he was annoyed by her feelings for him, and he replied, 'Why would I be annoyed?'

The soft hollow in Kouhouesso's neck, wide enough for her fingertips, as round as puckered lips: time unravelled inside that hollow. And she kissed him as if it was the last time; she clung to this man who was becoming a tree, impassive, silent and tall.

She was reminded of witch-pricking: the piercing of European witches all over their bodies in order to isolate the Devil's Mark, spots that were insensitive to pain, and thus proof of a woman's evil nature. The hollow in Kouhouesso's neck was like the last spot of softness in him. His softness had receded, almost to nothing, and was now lodged entirely in his neck—while everything in her was soft, vulnerable, undone.

*

He insisted: she should go to Poco-Beach, the Straight and Narrow really was a dump—actually that was *another* reason he visited her so infrequently. But she had no complaints: since he'd had chemical toilets installed, Little-Poco had become civilised.

Everything: he looked after everything. He was the boss, the skipper of the boat, the Coppola of Little-Poco. Every morning fifteen people were waiting in front of his hut with urgent questions: logistics, sets, props, water, schedules, a stolen paddle, a sudden altercation, the security firm treating the guards as slaves, departures, arrivals, returns, complications, crises. The distribution of wages, over the three filming locations, was done with envelopes of cash and a single courier on a motorbike, who had to be trusted. The Company had replaced Natsumi with a local wardrobe assistant, but Olga had got rid of her; as a result, she was overworked. The hairdresser, another local, was also doing make-up, without complaining: people here knew the value of work. The script boy had been recruited in Douala, the grips were from Nigeria, all the set workers and all the sound and lighting staff were Cameroonian. The allocated budget was phenomenal; the future of cinema was in Africa.

Kouhouesso strode purposefully through the forest: the trees were going to follow him as one, all in a row, directed at last. Machetes, secateurs, chainsaws and bulldozers: they were carving out corridors for the camera, otherwise the horizon loomed thirty metres away and the landscape closed in. The very idea of a film in that forest was a paradox that made Kouhouesso joyful and defiant.

THE NIGHT OF THE PANGOLIN

Favour was thinner and the size of her breasts had perhaps been enhanced. Draped in striped cotton fabric, her silhouette a slender S, she was batting her painted eyelids slowly. As if it was too much of an effort to bestow a glance on those who were not royalty. 'Brass leggings to the knees', gilded gauntlets to the elbow, two crimson spots painted on her cheeks—Olga and the hairdresser were fussing around her. Kouhouesso had bought, from a passing Bamileke man, a Gabonese Punu mask with a three-tiered hairstyle, and Welcome, the hairdresser, who was not Punu, or anything for that matter, was struggling to reproduce it in all its splendour on Favour's impatient head. Everyone was happy except her. There was the question of a wig.

That mask—almond-shaped eyes, long nose, imposing

forehead—it was her, Favour. Kou had an eye for it; it was unsettling. When she appeared on the riverbank, wearing 'the value of several elephant tusks' (plastic), all that junk, cheap tat, all those jumbled elements finally came together in a framed image, and it was stunning; it embodied something like the Big Idea, Favour raising her bewitching arms to the heavens.

The only ones Kouhouesso wasn't happy with were the men laying the rails: you would have thought they were French. The foreman was even a union member. They had huge problems uprooting stumps: deep holes had to be dug, then filled in with gravel transported from Douala. If they didn't uproot the stumps, suckers grew back within the hour, the river poured in, and the embankment collapsed; rails had been seen floating away. It was as if, at night, some indomitable force destroyed the day's work. It shook the earth, pulled up the sleepers. There was grumbling. Brows furrowed, eyes darkened at this curse on the deforested earth—naked and as if stripped. You didn't have to be a witch to hear rumblings reverberating around Kouhouesso, waves of sound around the centre of a gong.

All he could talk about was Godard's *Weekend*: the longest tracking shot in the history of cinema. He wanted his tracking shot to be subdued and smooth, as fluid as the river itself, stealthy, creeping along like the boat. He described the scene to the whole crew: the tracking shot would end with Favour raising her arms to the heavens. In the novel, her role stopped there, but there were rumours that she had wangled an appearance with George in the caves.

As for her, she could never find the right moment to speak to him about the Intended's scenes. She counted in days, like in Los Angeles: six days since they had slept together. The location scouting was dragging on; they were finalising Cassel's schedule first: they would fit in the minor scenes when they could. That's what the assistant director had told her.

*

An anteater. Sleepers in the water, disturbed soil: an anteater. They hung it by the tail at the entrance to Siphindile's. At one hundred and thirty centimetres and forty kilos, it was a good-sized anteater, the size of a ten-year-old child. Solange stayed on the verandah with the animal, which experts came to admire. They haggled. Its strange mouth, round and toothless, seemed to be sucking at the yellow dust. Solange was acquainted with moles, even big ones, from her mother's garden, but she had never seen anything like this.

Freeboy wanted someone to buy the whole animal. He had spoken to it as he was killing it, to ask permission; he would not let it be chopped up like a common porcupine. Patricien was the one who ended up with it, whole, for his wife's birthday in Kribi.

Fifty guests under a canopy of leaves, jerrycans of palm wine, musicians. The scales were the most difficult thing to deal with on the plate. Patricien said that anteaters were becoming extinct, that their scales were thought to be magic. One of the few non-human mammals to walk on its back legs, using its tail for support. Strictly nocturnal. Digs burrows, eats termites—its huge claws rip apart their towers, *crack*. Apart from that, it tastes a bit like duck, done with a peanut sauce confit.

Kribi was a pretty town. Patricien lived in a white wooden house, mouldy but nice. He was no longer poor, but he was not rich: no guard in front of what he called his 'residence'. Not far from there was the cathedral, the so-called French quarter, two or three colonial houses, a sort of casino and a rustic hospital, and then, of course, the inevitable huts, shacks and whatever. Patricien's wife had studied in Yaoundé. The hospital dated back to the nineteenth century, in every sense. There were interesting places to see. Perhaps things would be all right here for the Intended.

In the middle of the meal, she received a text message: 'Start without me.' He had finished with *K*, although he usually never signed off. How could there be any ambiguity? *K*, as if she could have been waiting for another man.

She drank yellow, frothy cucumber juice, ate fermented cassava, and the lump in her throat, the stupid knot in her stomach that she'd had since the days of waiting in Los Angeles, began to dissolve a bit. The sun was throwing confetti through the roof of leaves, and she could see herself from above, from the sky, from the satellites, a tiny dot among the other dots, drunk and a bit nauseated, in this little lagoon in front of the Ntem River, on the edge of the forest, deep in the Gulf of Guinea. Right in the crook of Africa. Far from the crook where she was born, the Bay of Biscay, the familiar right angle, smaller, more of an *alcove*, that she had left back in her own South-West.

Sitting here at this birthday meal, eating plantain banana and dead anteater, as if she'd been doing it her whole life. Kouhouesso had coloured her. He had turned her a little bit black. And the others knew it. She was becoming impregnated with their melodious accent, like in Clèves when she *got used to* men without education, women without careers, children without a future; but here she stayed vigilant because she was surprised by the responses. She thought hard. She made them repeat what they had said. She laughed belatedly at jokes and they found her charming. She was Africanising herself clumsily, but they forgave her. They were polite because they forgot that she was white. And she forgot, too. And she forgot K, a little. During the anteater party her mind was not preoccupied with him; he was everywhere but nowhere. She smiled at everyone. Wanting to be loved by everyone rather than by a single person was almost a relief.

PART IV

JUNGLE FEVER

The set designers had done a good job: you could have been in Europe. The 'mahogany door on the first floor' had not been at all difficult to track down: *ngollan* was not expensive here. For the marble chimney of a 'monumental white-ness' and for the grand piano 'like a sombre and polished sarcophagus', the set designer had, by default, opted for a sepulchral look. A side table, a patched armchair, the existing curtains, an imported rug: filming the Intended's scenes in the old casino in Kribi cost less than anywhere else. Very European, yes, except for the heat. She and Vincent tried to laugh about it, he in his suit and tie, she in her dress buttoned up to the neck.

She was overwhelmed with nerves. Not because of Cassel: she'd already worked with big names like him. It was Kouhouesso. That *connection* they had. She had always avoided affairs with directors. She had a pain in her gut. She was taking Imodium every day, as well as quinine infusions. Welcome and Olga were fighting. Welcome was irritable; the colours were running. If things dragged on, they'd have to start the whole thing again—they should have invested in air conditioning. And yet, acting out the cold was possible, like acting out Europe, or acting out sadness.

Olga seemed exhausted. And everyone called her 'The Chinese Girl', which infuriated her. The dress and the three-piece suit had never made it to Kribi. Perhaps they were floating in the middle of the Atlantic like debris from a shipwreck. The customs office at Douala operated like a filter, from where indispensable objects reappeared, or not. Olga had had to make another dress, find the appropriate material, dye it, starch it, get some little mother-of-pearl-like buttons made as fast as possible, dig up some lace from somewhere, cobble together a corset, and cut out a frock coat for Cassel from a fireman's suit.

And the light. The room was facing north, but there was flaring and the lighting engineers were having trouble. While he waited, Kouhouesso filmed small sections of the Intended's scene with a lightweight camera. He filmed her hands, resting on her knees that were draped in black. She saw them through his eyes: bare hands, pure white, bright blue veins. Welcome had given her a quick manicure… She surrendered her hands to him, the camera moved over them, it was gentle, it was good. Kouhouesso, all for her…

He was looking at her. He was filming her eyes. She stared deep into the lens. Bodies and shadows passed by at the edge of her vision. Welcome. Vincent. Lighting assistants. Set-design assistants, the assistant cinematographer. Kouhouesso was moving back, pulling away from her, and her eyes followed him, the light. The room was spinning, floating…Diaphanous blonde, halo of ash blonde. *Lights.* She was perfect for the role, it was made for her…*Camera.* Oh, she felt beautiful, and sad, and desolate. Her clear, smooth forehead illuminated by belief and love…'No one knew him so well as I…I had all his noble confidence. I knew him best…'

'Cut,' said Kouhouesso. 'We can't hear you.'

'No one knew him…He needed me…'

He was staring at her, scrutinising her. She would have liked to have more precise direction, for him to explain this man and this woman to her. For him to tell her the story of their love, tell her again about their betrothal…He kept her in the dark. In the blazing light. And the cameras were not filming, after all. The sun was annoying everyone. Cassel sat down again. Welcome put more powder on him. They started from the top.

'You knew him best…' Cassel was Marlow and himself at the same time, just like people speak two languages and come, self-evidently, from two places. In his reply was a hint of cruel doubt, a whole Congo of haziness; she and he had not known the same Kurtz…She had the impression of waltzing, but it was a desperate waltz. The light was worsening, all the efforts of the staff would not prevent the sun from rising…Action, action, Solange: 'I have been very happy—very fortunate—very proud…Too fortunate. Too happy for a little while. And now I am unhappy for—for life…' Tears filled her eyes, she was good, she was perfect, but Kouhouesso was not looking at her. Cut.

Instead of its usual grey, the sky flaunted blue depths and a parade of clouds. It flickered on the camera screen, like the light-and-shadow effect of Super 8. They could have been in the Île-de-France. Kouhouesso opened a window; the curtains blew; he inspected the sky as if waiting, from one rim to the other, for birds, omens, a gap in time that would last the length of the scene.

They were not there yet.

Around two o'clock, however, they were getting there, thanks to a big cumulus cloud that turned into a huge storm-filled sky, but which did not burst. They were running behind schedule; the convoy of four-wheel drives took them back in a whirl of dust—any pedestrian who did not get out of the way knew his fate, *yikes!* God's pencil does not have an eraser. They stopped at Little-Poco: they were dropping her off, picking up Favour on the way and leaving to film the scenes on the river.

Why didn't she go to Poco-Beach? She'd be much better off at Poco-Beach. They talked about it for five minutes out the front of Siphindile's. The heat was appalling. In the shade of the verandah they were haggling over monkeys. The little hanging bodies were stiffening without getting cold. At Poco-Beach she could be eating lobster.

Everyone was looking at them, both standing in the grey full sunlight. She said she would go there straight after Kurtz's death. Olga had made her yet another dress, a white one, for the scene in the caves. 'George loves it,' she assured him. Kouhouesso said nothing. He kissed her. For a long time, on the mouth. He held her gently by the waist and an electric current shot up the back of her neck. He left again in a four-wheel drive. For an instant, she stood there, stunned, her eyes seeing shadows where there were none.

The whole village had seen them kissing: it was official. Even if they had made headlines in the *Hollywood Reporter* her heart would not have been thumping this hard.

'Jungle fever,' said Siphindile. The girls starting laughing. It was a diagnosis: their saying for when a white woman wants a black man. And, sometimes, vice versa. The witch was at it, too: inoffensive laughter, as if none of it was too serious.

AND UNDER THE HUGE BLACK TREES

It had rained. The first downpours of the season. The track was so bad that they were all quiet, she at the back, clutching the doorhandle, anticipating the bumps and shivering, preoccupied by feeling cold in the brutal humidity. The winch cable broke the first time they got bogged. Like a rifle shot it sprang back, invisible, and left a long yellow gash in the trunk to which it was attached. The Toyota bounded forward, then stopped dead. She thought of the bulls from her childhood, of their final twitches on the ground.

Mud swallowed their boots. The Baka and Bagyelis guides, Freeboy, M'Bali and Tumelo, somehow managed to stay on the surface, wearing thongs. They all had amulets around their necks. Freeboy was constantly fiddling with his iPod and seemed to be murmuring prayers. Unless he was singing in his head. The forest was dripping, long cords of water; everything seemed vertical.

She felt dizzy. George gave her a bar of magnesium-enriched organic chocolate. George's agent had insisted on being there, as a kind of bodyguard, and it was weird having two extra white guys. George fitted in everywhere, whether it was desert, intergalactic space, urban jungle or here; but his agent was something else, with his explorer's jacket and his mosquito head net: all he needed was the helmet to look like Dr Livingstone.

They got the car started later. There were six of them in the large Toyota, which was now so steamed up that they couldn't see the forest anymore, followed by a whole convoy. The track was a dark tunnel. Patricien turned on the headlights. Kouhouesso said nothing. Patricien made conversation and George cracked jokes. She had a sore throat. She was obsessed by thoughts of hot tea. Her body ended up accepting the bumps as part of the habitat, a local manifestation of gravity. She became supple, elastic. She fell asleep clutching the doorhandle, groggy from the lurching, wedged between George and Freeboy.

They reached the ferry on the River Dja. The *mout-mout* sandflies were on the attack. Once she had put on her balaclava and her gardening gloves, the ferry boy (called 'the Admiral' by the pilot) stared at her more intently than if she had been bare-headed. The pilot and the Admiral laid two planks in the clay of the riverbank. Kouhouesso drove the first four-wheel drive, which embarked gracefully in one go. The little ferry subsided, the cables strained and the posts bent towards the water. Patricien held out his hand to her, George's agent made a point of holding George's hand, and they all climbed aboard. All at once, everything was simple; it worked. Things were running smoothly, without interruption. At last, time consisted of the same substance as the river. She had a Paris flashback: she was in Rue du Bac on the corner of the boulevard. Where was she headed? Who was she going to see? Back in her country. In the country where things flowed white. The Admiral leaned all of his little body over the enormous steering wheel and managed to turn it, faster and faster; the ferry lurched for a second, then edged forward, as if it understood what was expected, like a donkey or a horse. She felt the movement in her body. Then there was sliding. The ferry turned until it was across the river. And she said to herself, right, now it will get stuck somewhere and tip over. But no, the current made it go faster, side-on, like a crab.

The Admiral was scarcely more than a child. When she looked back at him he turned away, serious, his eyes fixed on the riverbank. Thousands of yellow butterflies fluttered, weightless, over the river. Kouhouesso was smoking, leaning on a Castrol tank, and she had another flashback, this time from when she was a little girl, of her father: such beauty, such strength, such total shutting down of oneself.

It was a cable ferry (at first she heard *clamp*). *Cable,*

the pilot corrected her, opening his mouth wide on the *a*. *Clunk clunk* all around them, a hullabaloo from hell, how old was this thing? From the Germans, for sure, the pilot reckoned: with an engine like that it had to be Prussian. He had inherited it from his father. In the very beginning there were elephants to crash through the forest and make elephantine tracks with their huge bodies. Behind them plunged duikers, antelopes, white-bellied hedgehogs, wild pigs, anteaters, bushbucks. And after them came the Pygmies, and after them the Bantu, and after them the white people: Germans, English, French. From his ferry, the pilot had seen elephants twice. Never any gorillas. What frightened him most were water buffalo, who stood their ground instead of fleeing. Once, he had seen a lion. In Douala, at the zoo.

She daydreamed about circus elephants. One walked past, with a red bellboy hat, straight out of her long-ago childhood, far from the jungles. But it was too late to go back to the past. To go back there, like going back to another country, was no longer possible: she was too far away, too embedded; nothing connected her to herself any longer, apart from this man, Kouhouesso.

He went back with the ferry; they had to do seven trips all up, for the seven cars and the whole crew. A thin line of mist veiled the middle of the river; Kouhouesso's silhouette turned grey, translucent. The ferry was silent in that direction, carried by the current or by something smooth and strange that she couldn't fathom. The *clackety-clack clackety-clack* only started up on the return trip, grew louder; the second Toyota arrived; everyone was wet; it was raining on the other shore. Then Kouhouesso set off again. Favour was in the final convoy. The four-wheel drive moved forwards on the water, the motor cut, as if carried by time itself. From afar, Solange saw Kouhouesso hold the door open and Favour climb out gracefully, her thin black arm raised to her mouth as he lit her cigarette. A puff of smoke. Only then came the *wham* of the door, only then the noise carried, reached her, three hundred metres a second, she calculated, three hundred metres a second if I screamed, if I called out his name, Kouhouesso.

Later, they drove along by a grove of oil palms, the sky aligned between the trunks. They reached the first cliffs. There was, unbelievably, a sort of car park. Baka women under a lean-to made of palm leaves were selling grilled fish. They were big fish, more like catfish, served whole in palm leaves, as takeaway. Further down there was a branch in the river where a man was fishing, using Ivory soap. The fish were crazy about it—whether it was the particular smell or animal fat, no one knew. She took a few photos. She watched M'Bali and Freeboy: they peeled off the skin with their thumbs; there were no scales. Crackled black skin over a layer of slimy fat; underneath it was good, yellow and juicy. She had removed her gardening gloves and little bees kept landing on her fingers—she let out a scream. It wasn't a sting, there was no stinger. Perhaps she had touched—what was the name of it—one of the antennae or whiskers of the fish.

'Those *soussous*,' said Freeboy, 'they stay alive when they're dead, *yikes!* When it's stuck on a spear it keeps moving for much longer-longer.'

Her thumb was swelling up. Trust her to get stung by a dead fish, a typical *moundélé*.[3] She had brought antihistamine cream, but her luggage was stashed somewhere in the Toyota.

They climbed on foot towards the caves. Between the trees, they could glimpse, not sky, but more trees, slopes full of them, at different heights. Freeboy pointed out huge round holes in the ground, elephant tracks, the clear imprint of their nails. M'Bali chopped off a double creeper and they tasted pure vegetable water. George's agent was the only one who refused it.

Occasionally, from behind, on the bends of the ascent, she glimpsed Kouhouesso at the head of the procession. They were moving fast. The path was clear, hardly any machete work needed. Since he'd been in the lead for so long, Kouhouesso was way ahead. Freeboy was running behind him and Kouhouesso seemed gigantic in contrast. Patricien brought up the rear; otherwise everyone was between her and Kouhouesso: Favour, Hilaire, Germain, Vincent, and George and George's agent, and Thadée, Idriss and Saint-Omer, and Kouhouesso, and Olga, M'Bali and Tumelo, Welcome, Archange and Pamphile, and Gbètoyeénonmon

---

3 Central African word for a white person, 'one who has come out of the belly of a fish'.

the Benin chef, whom everyone called Glueboy, and Freeboy, whom everyone knew by that name, which was probably his real name, and the MAS-36-carrying armoured guard, and others whose names she had forgotten. All these black people in single file, carrying things on their heads; it was all very well knowing it was for a film, that touch of déjà vu was still there. She and Favour were the only ones not lugging something along; even George and Vincent had backpacks.

Her hand was hurting and her forehead was burning, but she was also in the grip of something icy—the forest, she thought, the forest had a hold on her. She concentrated in order to keep walking. She said to herself: if I focus hard enough on Kouhouesso, he will turn around. He will turn around at the top of the path. He will turn around and look at me and wait for me. His head, with its unfathomable expression, will turn around. The hollow of his neck, so soft. And he'll smile at me and urge me on. No, just turning around would be enough. She launched the telepathic thread up the path. Kouhouesso was disappearing, swallowed up by the giant grasses. She headed towards him, sending powerful thoughts his way: turn around, look at me. But the line of walkers was stretching out and something on the path was blocking the way, the path was not cooperating, the path was against her. It was blocked at Favour. The forest and Favour were against her.

Out of the blue, the word came down that they were stopping, right there. An enormous fern, well, some green thing, a giant celery, had propagated to such an extent, via roots and new growth, that a platform had been created on the slope. Once they stopped, the little bees landed everywhere, bombarding wherever they could, as ferocious as flies. There was a flash: it was Favour nonchalantly throwing a sumptuous silvery stole over her shoulders. M'Bali wandered into the forest and came back with white worms he called 'cockchafers'. Bottles of water went up and down the line. The little chlorine tablets leaped as they fizzed: it was as if she was watching herself zigzagging, trapped, subdividing, diminishing. And, out of the blue, Kouhouesso. What was he doing? He was coming down the path. Where was he going? Further and further down the line. Why? He stopped in front of her. She raised her eyes. 'Are you all right, gorgeous?' She showed him her hand. He said it was nothing and squeezed it in his own hand. His lips shone. Had he eaten some cockchafers? Eat me, she thought. A prayer, a supplication to the cannibal. Eat me. Let's be done with it. Let him eat her forevermore.

WOMEN ARE IN THE FOREST

It was the silence of immense weariness. Silence around the caves. As for her, she was almost happy. Patricien looked worried. He was staring at the treetops—no, he was staring at Freeboy, who was staring at the treetops. Freeboy's lips were moving. They all knew that they should have got there before night-time, otherwise Freeboy and M'Bali and Tumelo, all the Pygmies, would refuse to go any further. Freeboy said the trees were talking. Patricien was translating. You could not see the demons, but they were there, and at night they came closer to the humans, at night they were unbelievably daring. Favour looked up at the sky. The demons got into people's mouths and made them utter prophetic, doom-laden declarations. They got into people's bodies and did the work of the devil.

'The trees are our source of information and advice,' said Freeboy. 'The trees are on the side of wisdom. The caves are sacred.'

Kouhouesso threw down his cigarette and announced that they were leaving. She was shocked: could they not wait and listen to what Freeboy was saying, what Patricien was translating and what the trees were saying?

Kouhouesso repeated, '*On y go. On y Johnnie, là.*'[4]

Freeboy shook his head. 'The forest is *bwi*.[5] The secrets have been exposed. The trees are suffering. Every tree chopped down exposes the tree left behind. Panthers break into the villages. The whole world falls ill.' But the main thing Freeboy was upset about—he was choking on his words; he seemed to be stammering, even if it was tricky for her to discern a stammer in a language she didn't speak—was that women were in the forest.

It's not just me, she wanted to object. Favour and Olga are here, too. Perhaps Favour and Olga are *bwi*, too?

'You're not Gabonese, are you, buddy?' asked Kouhouesso. 'The only people more superstitious than the Gabonese are the Corsicans. Come on, buddy, let's get going, otherwise the demons will be whistling in your ears.'

They set off, clambering over fallen trunks, holding on to each other's hands to get through the rocks. M'Bali and Tumelo got their machetes out again for the branches along

---

4   *Camfranglais*: Off we go. Let's hit the road.
5   *Camfranglais*: forbidden

the path. It was a long way. There had been storms; they hadn't thought to bring the chainsaw. Freeboy was sulking in the middle of the line. Soon there was nothing but a dazzling milky sky above their heads. The ground was drying out; the going was easier. They felt as if they had finally got the upper hand. The forest was laid flat, dominated; it was almost cultivated forest now. They could look down onto the trees, the wretched canopy, fleecy swathes of giant broccoli, the stalks poking through, along with the tops of artichoke and clusters of parsley. In the emptiness of her head, she found a scrap of herself to slip back on like an old hat.

She could stand straight, stretch, look around. But they had to keep climbing. She was trying to think of something to wish for, something for herself, other than Kouhouesso. Something that would remind her of wide open spaces, train stations and airports, solid ground, streets, fields. A childhood memory from where she could rewind herself. The afternoons in Clèves, summer, boredom. The carnivals and the elephants, yes, the elephants were there, too. Knocking their heads against the planks of their stalls, one night at the circus, her first kiss. Back in that past from which she was cut off by the forest. Time had been shoved into the trees and held there, in the forest. Time chopped into planks of wood for white people.

They reached a granite plateau. A last kapok tree, like a hand plunged into the rock. The sky was red. The men leaned against the deep furrows in the tree. Wings, curtains, between which they could lie. Kouhouesso had gone on ahead again, to the caves, to assess the location. M'Bali and Tumelo took off their backpacks and got out a flask of palm wine. Germain put down the generator he had been carrying on his head since morning, which had made him look like some kind of weird robot. Freeboy was biting into a whisky flask. The so-called white crew followed suit. A packet of Marlboro was passed round. Tents began to spring up. Hilaire got them collecting wood. Glueboy and Thadée lit a fire, ever so traditionally, with a cigarette lighter. George, Vincent, George's agent and Patricien were playing poker on a tree stump. Welcome was trying out some lipstick on Favour, who was attempting to dissuade him from whitening her skin. Olga was already asleep, her head against her costume trunk. They looked like a travelling circus that had got seriously lost.

All she longed for was to take off her boots and have a shower—that was it. It was dusk and the mosquitoes were attacking. She hid her face, the last square centimetres of bare skin, in her gloves. Kouhouesso had come back, his deep voice so recognisable. Problems with the location. M'Bali and Tumelo wanted to renegotiate their pay: night rate was more. Freeboy was translated by Patricien, their voices blended with Kou's voice. The rhythms of other languages. Bursts of laughter, then whispers. Off to sleep. Sounds all around her. Insects. The clatter of dishes on metal. Something banging on the ground. *Poof* as Quechua tents collapsed, laughter. Favour was calling out in English for something; then she was speaking in Yoruba on her personal Thuraya phone. Glueboy and Thadée were arguing in French: a bag of supplies was missing. The trees opened up and closed over. She could see Kouhouesso's back, further away, still further. Slowly, she parted the drooping branches. Her feet were sinking, she was sliding into the mud, subsiding.

She was woken by a kiss. Just like the butterfly kisses her father used to give her. She rubbed her hand over her hood and her glove caught something. A small animal—no, it was an insect. She shook the glove. The thing wouldn't come off. She decided to confront it. Kouhouesso would be proud of her. Round, bronze, multifaceted eyes. And perhaps two smaller eyes below. Four antennae, green and brown, the length of a long finger, thrumming. It stayed there, staring at her. Then it opened a sort of mouth and emitted a *hhhhiissss*, barely audible. With her two gloved hands she unhooked it and threw it as far as she could. Afterwards she shuddered for ages.

The negotiations had stopped. 'Palaver', he had explained to her one day, came from the Spanish: it was not an African word at all; it was a racist word. She thought of Lloyd in Hollywood, of his pitiless patience in business matters. In the meantime all the tents had been erected, even the big one with pegs. In a pale circle of light, Glueboy offered her something to eat. M'Bali had caught what looked like a furry child—a marmoset, Glueboy reassured her, as if it was more edible. She thought she could see hands in the pot. She sucked on a tube of concentrated milk. George brought her a tumbler of lukewarm coffee—it was the super-global brand for which he was the ambassador—'black, intense, rich, sensual and delicate'. They laughed like kids, out of earshot of Kouhouesso. Crickets were screeching at the tops of their lungs, assuming they have lungs, and something was hooting every now and again: an owl? The air was buzzing; animals were calling out to each other. In the end, they never actually saw any animals. Or only when they were dead. Insects and stars were what they saw. How refreshing to see stars. To inhabit the same planet as all those living things that could see the stars that night.

She moved off a few paces. The guys from the crew had chosen trees along the path. Favour, too—although Favour was probably not subject to any laws of nature. Solange walked around the kapok tree, which took about ten minutes. Showers of fireflies exploded at her feet, illuminating the undergrowth for a moment. The soil was clear, covered only with leaves. She remembered a television documentary about women collecting what looked like balls of wool from under a tree—handfuls of big grey spiders, to fry…But hang on, those women were Asian. They wore Chinese-style hats. In the watchful silence her stream of urine made the leaves crackle. She wiped herself with some baby wipes. She hesitated, then dropped them, right there on the ground. A slap in the face of Mother Nature.

She sprayed Rambo insecticide all over her clothes. The fireflies blinked, hello, goodbye.

She found Kouhouesso's tent. The flap was shut. She hesitated. She pulled on the zip gently and felt it slip out of her fingers: Kouhouesso, from inside, asked what she was up to, where had she been? She glimpsed his open arms in the darkness and cuddled up against him. She could not see him, which made it irresistible. He told her to take off her clothes: she stank of insecticide. The relief of bare skin. Yours, mine. He rolled on top of her; they breathed gently, trees and insects all around them, endless.

Afterwards, he talked. The structure supporting the central projector had been damaged in the storms and had to be reassessed before sunrise. And parts of the set were missing. Who would have thought light fittings and cables would be stolen? The guard posted at the caves had seen torches and heard singing; apparently he had left his post to have a closer look. Who would have thought fucking pilgrims would turn up in this forest? Later on, he called out in his sleep: could she stop moving? She was scratching herself. It was agony. Something had bitten or stung her on her buttocks and the tops of her thighs. She rummaged in her bag, trying to make as little noise as possible. At first the freshness of the baby wipes applied as bandages was a relief, then she wanted to howl, the burning pain was so bad.

All of a sudden, he sat up. His voice was harsh,

like a tree thrusting down into the earth: HE HAD TO WORK TOMORROW.

She lay still. The tormented hours before morning were like an abridged version of what she endured with him, yet another day of waiting, unbearable waiting.

A WORLD TOO PERFECT

They were on an island, a volcanic island that had appeared in the middle of the chaos. It was like looking out from a lighthouse. Threads of mist turning pink as the sun set. A huge population of trees, as thick as a sea of clouds, billowing, rippling, serried, of every shade of green, rounded, dome upon dome, laid out in a way that derived from nothing human, but rather from natural forms, the structure of growing things. There was Gabon, and then the Congo over there, the Congo where they would not be going. The sky turned completely red, then the light died. It was six o'clock. They could hear giants fighting, supernovas of leaves and dust and smaller trees dragged into the explosion, leaving holes in the ground. There was secret sawing going on. In the distance, was the sound of animals on the run, screeches.

They had not started filming yet. And George was leaving the day after tomorrow. They had had to rebuild the whole gantry for the lighting, redo a cable network and give up on the top light, which fused everything. The end result was a sort of wigwam of interconnecting wires with a projector on top and a reflector on the bottom, all of it inside the cave, as if the Pygmies had gone mad. When they had finally been able to connect the generator, a thousand bats flew off. And Kouhouesso had to make an announcement about how the Ebola virus was only transmissible if you were bitten.

Everyone was jittery, telling each other off, chasing after bits and pieces, running through the leaves, shrieking a bit like birds.

'Hey, Miss Chinese!' yelled Welcome.

'I'm Uyghur,' retorted Olga.

'Are you sick?' asked Solange anxiously.

'It's a nightmare,' said Favour into her personal satellite phone. They had located a large tree stump where the actors could wait. The wet moss was creeping up their backs; they felt themselves growing along with everything else. Seen from the trees, they must have looked like large mushrooms on a skewer. And the whole encampment in the clearing, entertainers among the chaos of green, was such an assortment of random and coordinated elements, thirty-odd human beings gathered together, bending over backwards to give shape to the Big Idea, conquering the

river, framing History and keeping the jungle in check...
and those characters would be seen moving around on
cinema screens far from here...Mushrooms were dangling
from her hood.

'You don't say "jungle",' said Kouhouesso. 'That's for
Asia. We're not in Mowgli country; anyway, there are no
tigers in Africa.'

His explanations of the world, in the three minutes a
day she managed to grab with him, were like stolen kisses.

While George and Vincent were talking poker, Favour
announced that it was scandalous: a so-called democracy
with a quarter of the French population not represented,
the quarter who voted for Le Pen and who were despised.
If the National Front won the election, at least the situation
would be clear, the truth would be out about the country of
the Rights of Man, and that's when we could start talking.
Solange tipped her head back towards the trees. She let
herself be carried along by the foliage. She wanted to go
home, home with him, back to their country, to a beach, a
house on stilts, a somewhere-else à la Laurent Voulzy, *under
the sun, we're all the same colour, the same colour for everyone, under
the sun*...

She swam in the river—barely a stream—where Hilaire
and Glueboy went to collect water. It was good to wash
herself, to sluice away the dust and sweat; as soon as she had
stepped in the lukewarm current up to her waist, it was as if
the heat of her body and that of the air combined, as if the

stream became heavy, too, constituted of the same matter as the forest. The animals remained mute. The birds were motionless. Even the insects were hiding; all she could see in the long grasses on the bank were little frogs, the size of a fingernail and glossy red. The water was marvellously clear; puffs of yellow sand rose between her toes. 'Come on,' she had begged Kouhouesso. He would not come.

She found the caves rather disappointing. Not so much caves as piles of fallen rocks, to be honest. Slabs that had slipped on top of each other and formed cavities. All right, it was attractive, and looked suitably haunted. Resin skulls were stuck on assegais; torches and spotlights did the rest, and all of the available black crew, including guides, cooks and grips—transformed into extras, wearing old-time fancy dress—were getting ready to clown around. Freeboy was the only one to baulk at the idea. Did they want to provoke the demons? Welcome chased after him to put his make-up on, the big Bantu on the heels of the little Pygmy; laughter rippled through the crowd like a whole lot of switches lighting up. Kouhouesso wanted mouths that would shine on film. 'As if their mouths were not already visible enough,' said Welcome, referring to the Pygmies.

Before the *clap* of the clapperboard, Kouhouesso made each person listen to the tone of *Heart of Darkness*, a few pages of the novel:

'The girl! What?...Oh, she is out of it—completely. They—the women, I mean—are out of it—should be out of it. We must help them to stay in that beautiful world of their own...'

Did the passages about women refer to her?

'It's queer how out of touch with truth women are. They live in a world of their own...It is too beautiful altogether, and if they were to set it up it would go to pieces before the first sunset.'

Kouhouesso was a literal man who knew about subjugation, who, like her, was conversant with the facts about domination. But no one objected, least of all Favour or Olga. It was a question of narrative, period, point of view...A last bat fluttered around without finding the exit: a low IQ. George went 'Boo!' as he shined his pocket torch beneath the bat; Freeboy did not laugh.

Freeboy's iPod never left his ears. Apparently it didn't work. Kouhouesso and Olga thought the dozen little trinkets attached to the earbud cords were wonderful. Pebbles, eye teeth, feathers, pearls and twists of string, what Kou called his *jujus*: wonderful, but best without the iPod. If Freeboy could just be sensible: keep his amulets, but on a leather cord. Otherwise the iPod would be visible on screen.

'*Je wanda*...who is this Kouhouesso? *Yikes*, does he grow Caterpillar machines? Does he eat hot pepper? Who does he think he is. The man is full of himself! Don't get me started. Whatever, whatever, I have to speak up now. I wear my things and he wants to use them? *Hell!* This guy looks really really bad. *Helele*, what's he talking about? It's a lie!

What a sycophant. I've got a bone to pick with him. I don't give a fuck! He's stirring up shit with me. I'm walka me. What a green dog. What a lying cheat, that's it. I'm outta here, pardon!'

Patricien translated Freeboy's *camfranglais* in the neutral tone of an interpreter from the United Nations. So Kouhouesso's authority was in doubt; persecution had its limits. Freeboy pulled out of the project.

He rolled up his sleeping mat, took some flasks of whisky, some sticks of cassava, his scrap of soap and his scrap of towel, tied it all up with a creeper, and headed into the forest. The sound of his machete echoed for a while, then died away. Freeboy had a flair for the dramatic. Fortunately there were still a couple of Bagyelis guides, M'Bali and Tumelo. But absolutely no one could understand a word they said.

She put on the long white tunic Olga had laid out for her. Welcome had made her up with a pallid complexion, a bit too vampire for her taste, but she would only make a hazy appearance. George-Kurtz was on his deathbed, and the Intended wafted before him. It was her idea—taking liberties with Conrad, but he could go to hell. In front of the spotlights, the insects gathered in clouds so dense you could see them, their buzzing so loud you could hear them. They had to use the fan to drive them away, but without it being visible or audible. Favour, that schemer, was also in the scene, as flamboyant and wild as Solange was pale and languid; one had to wonder if Kouhouesso wasn't falling for the very clichés he wanted to condemn. She glanced at the video-assist screen: it looked good, anyway. She adjusted her tunic one last time: it was her good side. She leaned forward slightly to get in a better light. Watch out: lights, camera, action.

CAMEO

Those words he had said to her. 'See, it's not working.' He had turned to her at the end of the last take. She felt as if the words had made their way into her forever, as if she would hear them over and over in the silence. See, it's not working.

And yet the scene was beautiful. She was standing straight, ghostly, soulful. But he said that he didn't believe in it. That Kurtz's final thoughts were not about the Intended. That all Kurtz wanted was to 'exterminate all the brutes'.

They made love. Let's call it love. At first it seemed like he didn't want to. But as soon as he touched her…Perhaps, also, he was astonished, confused, mystified. They were radiant, intoxicated, in awe. They both plunged beneath their skin. One shudder after another. Stripping back, layer after layer, a little more, a little further, until they reached the skeleton, the universal whiteness of bone, in the universal blackness of flesh.

He was so tired. George was flying back tomorrow. All the close-up shots were in the can, but for the end of the film, well, Kouhonesso would use a mannequin or a body double to set up the scenes where Kurtz's corpse is carried on board the boat. He was talking to himself. His hands were moving like moths. He might as well take the role himself, a Hitchcock appearance, a cameo. He would appear, then disappear, dead, stiff, a cadaver; they could whiten his hands and substitute George's head in the editing. Cinema language was all he used now: these were becoming his everyday words. She wondered if he was taking amphetamines or something. Words of love were the words she was speaking, softly, her head in his neck, in that nocturnal, salty hollow. Was he annoyed by her feelings for him? Why would he be annoyed…She mouthed *I love you*, breathed *I love you*.

Words. The substitution. The editing. The Intended. She saw strange bodies. Creatures from films. Ancient monsters, Blemmyes, whose heads were in their torso and who were said to be cannibals, the Nubians seen by the first white explorers. See, it's not working. She saw the child on the ground, in the witch's hollow tree. She felt her forehead burning but she was cold: two climates had a hold over her, a chronic malaria and a drowsiness that was all her own. He was taking the time to explain the film to her again, even though time was running out for everything.

But he did not know on the last night. He did not know himself that it was their last night. She was certain of that: now the film was finished, he was not making any plans. She herself did not know; no one knew that was it, their last night.

*

That was the end of the film shoot. There was a party for the men at the Kribi casino. The next day he was not to be seen. Perhaps he was not even in his hut; she couldn't hear the fan. And the guard had left, disappeared, gone back to the forest.

Perhaps she knew. Of course she knew. That there would be no more nights. It was obvious from the fact that she went walking on the beach the following day. Poco-Beach— the name is meaningless. The local name is Mohombo. Paradise, coconut palms and smooth sea, a potholed road. He had told her that he would take her there, but he had stayed on the river; no one could get him to leave that boat. There was a spot for her in one of the pick-up trucks with Welcome and Olga, and Hilaire and his family, Germain and his sisters, and M'Bali, his wives and his children, but not Tumelo, who could not be found. It was all being dismantled, already. Welcome and Olga could no longer stand each other. But Welcome was not even calling her 'Miss Chinese' anymore; he looked depressed. Bits of the set turned up, they were taken to pieces, sent away, resold, stolen, shared around. It was all coming to an end; the different orbits were set in motion again: Olga off to another film, Vincent to Singapore, the Africans staying put. She was heading in the direction of Kouhouesso. Welcome was returning to Lagos, to the Nollywood studios, where he would find work. As for the others, who could tell? The fate of a homosexual make-up artist in black West Africa—who could tell?

Equatorial Guinea was a green line under the rain. The river was wide here, shimmering, and the rain was a speck over there. The Ntem River was nicknamed the Little-Congo. Still, it was not the Congo. A motorised canoe, loaded fit to sink, was carrying a pyramid of fuel barrels. A single shot from Guinea and the guy would disintegrate, for the equivalent of—she mused, her head empty—what must be the cost of the perfume she had given her mother for Christmas. The film crew got their supplies through him. Otherwise there was nothing, nothing at all. The mangroves seemed to have been coated halfway up their roots in some white pesticide mixture. At the low-tide area, the silt beach was cleared beneath the sentry box of the customs official who spent his days here, alone. It designated the centre of Poco-Beach, as it were. The central business district, let's say. He liked to chat, understandably. He had not been paid for two years, and did a bit of wheeling and dealing in butane on the side.

The sea was in the shape of a wave, beneath the horizon, at the point where the green receded. A grey-white rip current. The mouth of the river, the Earth opening up, the whole expanse extraordinarily wide and flat, spreading, held back from non-existence by a few suspended molecules. On this side, the encampment of Nigerian fishermen. On the other side, the sea, shacks, the silt turned to sand, the mangroves turned to coconut palms. She stirred up spider crabs and sand fleas with every step.

The rain was moving in, the rain from the equator. There was a rainbow like a whale's spurt, forming a bridge over to Guinea. One day, a long time ago, she had given a book to her son, at her mother's place, a book about a little travelling rainbow. He had never wanted her to read it to him. Her mother had told her that it was a bit childish for a ten-year-old boy. Here the sun rose every day at 6.18 a.m. precisely, and set exactly twelve hours later, at 6.18 p.m. Nights as long as days. An eternal equinox. It would drive you crazy, she thinks.

Poco-Beach, on the side with the shacks, was a scrap left over from the Africa of the film shoot: three bungalows that were almost elegant, a canteen on stilts, almost-western toilets, an isolated beach. There was a bit of money left, for a small party; the luxury four-wheel drives would be returned tomorrow in Douala; the more valuable material would be loaded into containers for Hollywood, via Panama. Jessie had left ages ago. The big shindig was over. Now it was time for the Africans to party.

POCO-BEACH

She was walking; there she is walking on the beach. While the meal was being prepared. Years later, there is still a photo, taken on her iPhone by Olga. It was the beginning of photos sent by phone: a slender figure, long legs and a small bust, in a blue and gold Hermès sarong, a big straw hat, Chanel sunglasses, bare feet. In the end, it could have been anyone, any old white person of childbearing age, wearing high-end fashion accessories and corresponding to the beauty criteria of the year 2008. An ad for Poco-Beach. Ten minutes later she went for a swim. He had just arrived. She wanted him to see her, for him to say again 'a real little fish'. After leaving her sarong on the sand with her hat and glasses, she dived into the waves. She was wearing her pretty bikini. She was the only one swimming. A game of beach volleyball was starting up. Everyone was in their swimming costumes except Olga, who was staying out of the UV rays.

Welcome, in swimming shorts, was good-looking but odd. From a distance, you couldn't help noticing it: unlike most human beings, his face was lighter than the rest of his body. He was two-tone. Skin-whitening creams. A fake Michael Jackson look.

M'Bali was making gestures, difficult to interpret but somewhat alarming. '*Mami wata*,' he said. Sharks? Opposite, on the horizon, there was only the oil rig and the surveillance boats around it. Germain, Hilaire, his wife and children, Welcome, Saint-Omer, Kouminassin, Abou, Glueboy, Thadée, Favour, Idriss, and Ignatius of the blowpipes, and even Patricien's wife studying in Yaoundé—it was as if they were all on hold, in slow motion on the beach. *Mami wata*, no one was happy about it. The spirit of water, lascivious and feminine, which wants all of you and takes it. Before swimming, you had to exorcise the spirit of the sea. Kouhouesso was laughing. All the same, he didn't come in for a swim. She returned to the water's edge. She remembered Malibu, the illusion that he was hers: come on, *splash*, in the water, come on, Kouhouesso, *splash* in the setting sun... He pulled his arm away; stop it, he said—so cold, so sharp. She realised he did not know how to swim.

There was a screening of the rushes. As if performing an exorcism, the Bagyelis made gestures at the images portraying their own deaths. Afterwards, everyone laughed, everyone drank. There were some leftover blowpipes. They had a mock battle, harmless arrows rained down. Fish on the grill. Palm wine flowing. They chewed on kola nuts and drank beer. The sun set directly over the oil rig and the sky blazed. A huge sound system had been brought in from Kribi, but the electricity kept cutting out, the same phrase of music was on repeat, *kiri kiri mabina ya sika,* the catchy, sad guitar of Docteur Nico was the essence of the Congo, the lost Congo of the rumba, of the merengue, all the things she knew absolutely nothing about and to which Kouhouesso had led her, and, melancholy, they danced barefoot in the sand, in their ideal Africa, their Africa of coconut palms, of black people all together, of kind white people, with Asia, with Olga, with America and cinema, and petroleum flowing like water without oil spills, gold and ivory decorating palaces without genocides, and diamonds sparkling on girls' fingers, all girls, an Africa where everyone loved each other, and danced, with Welcome and his painted mouth, come on friends, *kiri kiri mabina ya sika,* the Africa of electric guitars with wah-wah pedals, the Africa of Hawaiian shirts, of Sapeur-suited fashionistas and high-heeled shoes, the post-independence Africa photographed for all time in its stucco sunlight, the Africa of the band, African Fiesta.

The film shoot was over. The Africans were looking into the distance. Gazing offshore, as if witnessing their own absence in countries where they had no place. That was all it was, in the end, a film; it was already over. Back to disappointment. The future did not last long. Eight weeks of eating protein every day, eight weeks to gain another eight weeks, two months of future for the village, sacks of rice and palm oil. Kouhouesso had left them a Toyota and a generator, and diverted some Company money to pay for typhoid vaccines, twelve euros for the vaccine times one hundred and fifteen children, and as many boosters in a year, which could be stored at the right temperature, or not, in Siphindile's fridge.

'To be African has no meaning, except to be frightened of losing what you have.' Kouhouesso was drunk. He was hugging her but he was also hugging Olga. He said, 'It's okay, girls.' He said, 'How will we do it? Do you fancy a threesome?' The way he spoke, she heard *treesome*. More tree business? Olga got angry, so she realised it was a proposal for the three of them and, even knowing he was drunk, she felt hurt, yes. She felt like crying. Favour was the one who had retained her dignity; she was looking at them with her superior air, with the same look as on the first day: unscathed, untouched. Favour Abebukola Moon. A future star. There was no escaping it.

Patricien was not dancing. Patricien was not drinking. There had been…an incident. On the track heading towards the rubber plantation, in one of the displaced-persons camps. A little girl had been hanged. The mother had died giving birth to the newborn boy and the little girl, six years older, had been accused of devilry. One group of camp inmates, against the wishes of the rest, had hanged her by the feet to extract a confession. She had been left there, dangling from a rubber tree. A cousin ran to tell Siphindile; he ran across the whole plantation, ignoring the guards, straight through the rows of trunks. Siphindile told the witch, who said, 'I don't get involved with those people.' He ran to see the only official in his sentry box on Poco-Beach. He even tried to find Kouhouesso, but he was not on the boat or answering his phone. When he found Patricien, who knew the Kribi police, it was too late. And anyway, those people in the camps—they are violent-violent, those people like problems, *yikes.*

*

In the plane on the way back she read the French papers. The Angoulême museum had reopened. Sebastien Loeb had won the Rally Mexico in a Citroën C4. The city of Lyon was celebrating the bicentenary of Guignol. A large cannabis network had been shut down in the Saint-Étienne region. A high-school student of African origin who stabbed his female teacher had been imprisoned for thirteen years. The Brown Western Spadefoot toad had been declared an endangered species. For the first time a woman was president of the board of directors of the École Polytechnique. A public prayer of reparation was recited by militant anti-abortionists outside Timone Hospital. The court case concerning human growth hormones was continuing. Idriss

Deéby, in Chad, pardoned the French charity workers who had falsely claimed a number of children were orphans. A Chinese freighter carrying 4300 tons of tropical wood from the Congo had been intercepted off Ouistreham. On the internet, a social network called Facebook, driven by its American success, had launched in France. A French paracetamol manufacturer was moving offshore, to India. Lazare Ponticelli, the last survivor of World War I, had died at the age of 110. The Greens had lost half of their votes in Paris. The disabled community of France were demonstrating for a pension increase. According to a survey run by the Catholic church in the region of Nîmes, 44 per cent of the respondents said they did not necessarily believe in God, 65 per cent thought that one can be a Christian without belonging to a particular church, and 56.5 per cent maintained that God existed. The Chtis community claimed it was insulted by a banner displayed during a soccer match in Lens. Alain Bernard beat the world 50-metre freestyle record. The social security deficit was not increasing. In Cherbourg, Nicolas Sarkozy unveiled the construction site of the nuclear submarine *Terrible* (weight 14,200 tonnes, length 138 metres, diameter 12.5 metres, maximum speed 25 knots). Gold was trading at $1000 an ounce. The parents of Maddie, the girl kidnapped in Portugal, proclaimed their innocence. A senator from Illinois, Barack Obama, won the presidential primary in Mississippi. A Japanese satellite was sent into orbit by the space shuttle *Endeavour*. Bombings in

Russia. Riots in Yerevan. Violence in Sudan. Elections in Malta and in Sri Lanka. A base camp was swept away in the Himalayas, a survivor reported: 'All of a sudden it was dark. I realised we must be under an avalanche.'

At Roissy she was shocked by the countless number of white people. Soft, pink, speckled skin, plucked chickens, walking serious-serious.

There she is collecting her bags, the correct label: all the bags look the same. There she is pulling on a big sweater. It's April and she's shivering. There she is walking towards the line of taxis. She is going to have a rest at Daniel and Lætitia's place; there will be fresh bread on the table, baguette; the little Christmas tree will have been dismantled. Then she will take the train to Clèves and recharge her batteries, as they say, with her parents and her son.

PART V

THE END

She got dressed in a flash. She had known forever that she would wear her blue lamé sheath, a vintage Dior from the seventies, the most beautiful item in her wardrobe. Forever, since the beginning, since the first mention of the film, and even when she didn't believe in it, she had seen herself at the premiere in this sheath. She had seen herself in this sheath on his arm.

She was swimming in it. She had lost a lot of weight since their separation. They lived in the same city but he had remained immersed in his project, preoccupied with his editing, deep in the teeming river of his film, in his teeming river, over there somewhere, making no contact whatsoever, and when her messages became more like pleas he sent a final text, one of his one-liners that took her breath away:

'You have to turn the page, Solange.'

Solange. He called her Solange. Right until the end, in her mind, that would be their secret.

Afterwards, nothing. News via other people. She was not waiting for anything anymore, other than the premiere. Stopping waiting became another life, breathable and sad. And now she was concentrating on how to put on the sheath without damaging the lamé. She pretended as if the only thing that mattered from now on was wearing a dress.

Her hairdresser opted for a nicely textured chignon, deceptively loose on the nape of her neck. She closed her eyes; the urge to cry came over her again.

She sent a limousine to collect her father and her mother and her son at LAX. She was putting them up in a hotel. It was too much to have them at her place. She left them with Olga to find something stylish at Vanessa Bruno and Paul Smith on Melrose (her mother would have wanted to *rent dinner suits*). Most importantly, she had managed to convince Rose and her husband to come—she had sent them two plane tickets. And Olga was coming with her. She needed Olga. The poster featured only George and Vincent, and some trees and a river. Well, Favour wasn't on it, either.

On the ivory and gold invitation card in the shape of a tree, the venue of the premiere was listed as the Chinese Theatre on Hollywood Boulevard. Before leaving, she downed a few whiskies, perhaps one too many, as confirmed by the *Hollywood Reporter* online videos: she seemed to hesitate as she stepped out of the limousine; if you looked carefully, she staggered a little, by herself, on no one's arm. Her son and her father were walking behind, then her mother, then Rose and her husband, then Olga and her boyfriend. Red carpet, random camera flashes. She was looking around (you can make that out from the video, too) for a welcoming look. Ted. Or even Lloyd, despite their disagreements. Not one of the Africans was there, not Patricien, or Glueboy, or Hilaire, or Ignatius, or Freeboy, obviously. Things were back to normal: almost all the world was white.

Welcome: she missed his expert make-up brush, his straightened hair and his poor person's dream of white skin. How old was Welcome? Twenty? The same age as her son. The only thing she knew for sure was that she would never see him again. Back there, down in Poco, down in Kribi, perhaps the invitation cards were decorations on the dried-mud walls. Perhaps they had landed, through some miraculous journey, inside the palm-leaf hut of one M'Bali or of one Tumelo, if those huts were still standing, stuck between the rubber plantations and the palm-oil groves. Perhaps they had landed on the mirror of Welcome's make-up table, somewhere in Lagos, if Welcome was still alive. Perhaps the Company had sent the invitations; perhaps Kouhouesso had thought to arrange it. But without goody bags, without plane tickets or visas.

She waited for the new press attaché, deep in conversation with Oprah, to come over and say hello. They raved about her sheath, then, looking around, raved about the Chinese-style decor that they knew inside out. They talked about George, who was filming in Berlin with Steven. And about Vincent, who was, such a pity, in Japan. They were waiting for Jessie.

George's agent completely ignored her, as if he didn't know her at all. He had always regarded her from the perspective of a man for whom passion, in a woman, at whatever level it might be, professional or romantic, is an inappropriate demonstration of feeling. As if, in this whole story, there had been, on her behalf, a lack of taste, immoderate behaviour, an unacceptable crossing of boundaries. There was a rumour that, in the forest, he had caught a debilitating parasite, the type that enters through the soles of your feet.

Father, mother, son, Rose, Rose's husband, Olga, Olga's boyfriend—she sat in the middle of the kebab skewer, row fourteen on the left. Floria arrived, magnificent, followed by Lilian in her hat. She stood up, disturbing the whole row, to go and give them a kiss. Still no sign of Kouhouesso. The evening was running late. There was a commotion, Jessie was arriving, with Alma. Two years later, who would have thought? In the chaos, she had managed to end up, standing, a few rows further ahead. She bobbed up and down, laughing loudly, trying to catch Jessie's eye. Then she climbed back up to her seat, disturbing everyone all over again.

In the meantime, Kouhouesso appeared out of nowhere.

He kissed Jessie and Alma, back down where she'd just come from. He waved, perhaps at her, no, more towards the centre of the theatre.

He was alone. Extremely handsome in a leather suit and an open white shirt. The only thing she didn't like was his hair, re-braided American-style, the braids right on the scalp. Welcome would have done better.

She scarcely heard the speeches—from Ted on behalf of the Company, from Oprah, from Kouhouesso. She listened out for her name—in the thanks, perhaps? Jessie went up on stage, applause. And Lola! Lola Behn was in the first row. The Lola from Suriname. What was Lola doing there? Kouhouesso returned to his seat between Jessie and Oprah, and just before the lights went out she caught sight of the top of his head, the braids in perfect ridges. She wondered if he still smelled of incense; she was even convinced of it, from this far away...*Oh, she knew him well, no one knew him so well as she*...She was certain that beneath that skull not a single thought slipped away from the screen, away from the night, from London and the Thames and the schooner at anchor, and the men's voices and the sooty shadows, then the immense light of the African coast, the sky so much bigger than the Earth, the sea the colour of zinc, the white foam far off on the reefs, and like foam, the green moss, of trees, of mangroves, and like a gushing of grey milk, the mouth of the river, making its appearance, infiltrating deep into the ocean, the river navigable right from the ocean, Africa wide open well beyond its coastline, everything she hadn't seen looking from the plane from Douala and that she saw right there, from the water, from her seat in the fourteenth row and from all her missing of him, right there, fourteen rows further down, perfectly locatable in the darkness of the cinema, and invisible, and apart.

Then the boat. 'A continuous noise of the rapids…' It became, how should she put it, more distinct; she recalled some of the rushes. The editing was phenomenal; she was overwhelmed by the sensitivity of it, his sensitivity, when he was sensitive—as well as the violence within that sensitivity. The film she saw was what remained of the film, its milky, churning surface. The film she saw was the memory she would have of it: what was being etched into her memory, seamlessly, without time passing. She would remember forever being there, fourteen rows from him, caressing the screen with her eyes. She was remembering already, as if it was her own past.

She tried to reactivate her critical faculties. To see if there was anything not quite right. Something was not quite right, but what? Was it an issue with the pacing? Did it lose dramatic tension? She should have been on the screen. Now. Emerging. White dress and arms outstretched. '…Her and him in the same instant of time…' She was not emerging. The white shape that she should have been. 'This eloquent phantom.' The phantom, no one. Her voice, lost.

Olga took her hand and the warmth of her skin held

her there, enclosed, in the fourteenth row.

George, his ivory face among the torches. The forest. Then the body of someone else, of Kouhouesso, carried on board, the white face, eyes shut, carried... *Cut,* and it was convincing, yes, no one knew, no one could tell...

The beats were missing from her heart. The forest was coiling like a mirage, never thinning, never diminishing, hurtling all at once to the sea, yes, it was the sea and she was not there. A Congo for the movies, the mouth of the Ntem River transplanted as if the planet had been refashioned, a better model, more practical, telluric plastic surgery, the Chinese Theatre on Hollywood Boulevard.

Why weren't they in 'Europe'? Where were the scenes shot in Kribi? Where was she? Where had she been left; in which pixels had she got stuck? Why was the music fading and the film ending and why were the words *The End* appearing in cursive script, like in the old days, like in the old movies: why bother with the words when it's already over?

Applause, deafening applause over her absence. She was not there. She was not in the film. Murderous lights. Her three scenes were missing. Even Olga was getting agitated. Perhaps there was a glimpse of her...the ash-blonde halo... the vampire pallor...Kurtz said, 'The horror! The horror!'... and perhaps you could make out a white glow, some kind of retinal impression...No. He had cut out every trace of her. And she had summoned them all here—her father, her mother, her son, her friends. Imperious, she had organised everything, bought the plane tickets, arranged their seating, right here, in order to witness her absence.

'It's because of your dress,' whispered Olga. 'They were hideous, those dresses.'

'What a beautiful film,' said her mother. 'But I didn't see you, darling?' And she hugged her and said, 'It was really good. It was really good anyway, darling. Sweetheart.' And the fourteenth row stood up, the cinema emptied, emptied out her blood. Kouhouesso, right there, his head ridged with parted hair. She remembered the beautiful, serene head in the loft in Topanga, the King of Ife, not a woman but a king. And she was the thread he had undone, a character easily unspooled from the film, who is not missed, a ghost who does not leave behind the outline of her absence: she was unnecessary and everyone was in raptures, and Kouhouesso would go to Cannes and to the Oscars, without her, snip go the scissors.

AFTERWARDS

Afterwards there is a cocktail party, a crush of people, and she has to have a drink, quick, champagne. And he comes over to see her; he is walking towards her. She immediately raises her hand, refusing. He can keep his upset look to himself. And yet they're together. It's astounding. He has inched forwards, crossed the threshold, the circle of ashes, and now they have entered the same sphere. That gesture she made—putting out her hand to stop him, her open palm, vertical, raised—she would never have made that gesture to anyone else; that decisive, familiar gesture is for him: she knows him. Oh, she knows him well. And the way he looks at her: he looked at her like that in the canyons. When the coyotes were howling. And later in the forest. Among the swarms of fireflies. The sea and the forest: he looks at her like he looked at them. She does not know why. But what she does know—if he comes any nearer, she will die. There will be nothing left of her but powder. Nothing but a blur. If he touches her. She will disappear. If he talks to her; even one word will be enough.

EXTRAS

Years later, almost ten, at another cocktail for another premiere, Jessie is the star this time, Favour is there, perhaps Gwyneth, George is there, and he is there. She is about to turn forty-six but she has worked with Soderbergh, with Malick, with Michel Gomez, with Nuri Ceylan, with Kaurismäki.

He has cut his hair short. She recognises him immediately, of course, but he is no longer quite the same man. He smells different now. The air between them, when they enter each other's respective spheres, thickens and heats up, and the vibration of the air is tiresome, but she breathes and holds her own. *Heart of Darkness* was released on DVD Director's Cut. One day she found it in her letterbox: the scenes of the Intended had been incorporated, but in the

Extras section. The rumour is that he left Lola after the film's success. That he had a short fling with Bianca Brittany, and that he was devastated by the suicide of the young star. Tonight he is with an amazing creature, half-Canadian, half-South African, the one who was in *Battlestar Galactica*. It seems he's writing a film for her.

He opens his hands in surprise, he pretends awkwardness; they kiss each other *à la française*, on both cheeks, firmly. They laugh. They have a glass of champagne each. Another. It's crazy, how their friendship is still so close. The affection as well as the resentment. *Whatever, whatever*, companionship. Companionship despite everything, two survivors of the same odyssey or, let's not go overboard, of the same bumpy journey. They end up speaking French, he in his deep, mellow voice, and she takes on his smooth, humming accent. In the end it's affection, from a past long ago-long ago: she has known him forever.

He tells her about a sort of illness he had. 'I have never forgotten you. For three years, after the film, I never found a single woman who came close to you. Yes, for *three* years, there was not a single woman I liked as much as you.' And from his matter-of-fact, admiring, kind tone, she knows that it is the most beautiful declaration of love that he will ever make to her.

NOTES

The epigraph by Marguerite Duras is from *Practicalities*, translated by Barbara Bray, Harper Collins, 1990 (from *La Vie Matérielle*, Éditions P.O.L., 1987).

The lyrics by Josephine Baker are translated by Penny Hueston.

The proverb on p. 193, 'Only people without a vision resort to reality' is cited by the South African photo-grapher Santu Mofokeng in his book *Chasseur d'Ombre*, Prestel, 2011.

The quotations from Aimé Césaire are from the translation of Aimé Césaire's *Notebook of a Return to My Native Land* (*Cahier d'un Retour au Pays Natal*), translated by Clayton Eshelman and Annette Smith, Wesleyan University Press, 2001.

Marie Darrieussecq received a Stendhal Travel Grant from the Institut Français for the writing of this novel.